Body Swap

Book 1

Catastrophe

Katrina Kahler

Copyright © KC Global Enterprises Pty Ltd

Table of Contents

Hiding

```
Jack, R U alrite?
```

That was the first text I got from Tom, my best friend. I peeked out from under the comforter to read it, then wrapped the blanket around my head again without replying. I wasn't in the mood to deal with him right now. I wasn't in the mood to deal with *anyone*. I just wanted to lie in the dark and pretend I didn't exist.

The cell phone buzzed again. I sighed.

I made a little hole, just large enough for my eye, and stared angrily at the phone. I wanted it to realize what it was doing was wrong. That I wanted to be *left alone*. The phone stared back at me, a small notification light flashing on the top of the device. I picked it up and looked again.

```
R U there? I heard U askd Jasmine 2
the dance! R U crazy??? D: )-:<
```

I *wished* I was crazy. That would have made everything so much simpler. When I retreated back into my cave this time, I tried putting my pillow on my head too, hoping that it would stop the sound of the phone from cutting into my solitude. I closed my eyes as tightly as I could and tried to wish everything back to normal. That works sometimes in the movies, right?

BUZZ BUZZ.

"Agh!" I jumped slightly as the phone somehow buzzed even louder this time (how did it *do* that?) and the pillow flew off my head. Sunlight shone in through the window, blinding me. I squinted and waited for my room to blur into focus. The white walls, my posters of awesome superheroes, my laptop, my guitar... I grumbled as I leaned over and looked at my phone screen again.

Wat abt HOLLY? UR GRLFRND? Ppl are sayn she is v. upset!

I threw the phone down on my bed. It bounced twice and ended up balancing on the edge of the mattress. I didn't blame Holly. I was also v. upset. A few weeks ago, my life had been pretty much *perfect*. I had the hottest girl in school as my girlfriend, I was a star player on the football team, I had a band that was definitely going to be famous someday soon, and it was *all* going my way.

Now it was all gone, swirling towards disaster. Actually, disaster was a while back. Now things were definitely swirling towards complete chaos.

My life was destroyed and I was hiding in my bed.
That *doesn't* happen in the movies.

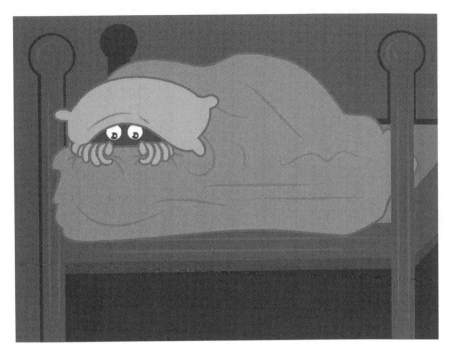

My phone buzzed again.

`This is a jk, rite?`

A joke. That's a good way of describing it. My life
was a complete joke. I had no idea what to do.

What happened? Let me explain.

The Unbeatable Plan

It all started a few weeks earlier. You know when you are having the *worst* day ever? Where everything goes wrong, no matter how hard you try? You trip over the smallest thing, you spill drinks all over your clothes, you seem to have somehow forgotten how to act like a normal human being? Well, it was one of those days, only times a *million*. No, actually *ten million. A million hundred million!* (Is that even a number?) Never mind, I'm just trying to say it was *really* bad.

It started off like any other day. Another *boring* day at *boring* school. It was a particularly *boring* day because I had the lesson I am worst at: Math. As usual, it was a disaster. Mr. Thomas, my grumpy, goblin-like Math teacher, yelled at Tom and me for '*talking when we should be learning*'! I tried to tell him that we were 'discussing the problem' (we were actually talking about our favorite candy, but how could *he* know?) and that 'learning was very important to us' (I stole *that* line from my Dad), but he wasn't having any of it and made us stay late afterwards to do *more* Math work.

When Tom and I left, I had to hurry. After all, today was the day I was going to put my **plan** into action.

"You sure you're ready to do this?" Tom asked as we rushed away from the classroom, ducking and dodging past anyone who got in our way. If you saw us both, you'd think Tom was the bravest: after all, he was as tall as most teachers and looked a bit like a tank with a flash of blond hair on top. But really it was little ol' me who dared to push the boundaries of awesome.

"Oh yeah," I grinned. "The **plan** is foolproof."

What was my **plan**?

Well, you see, today was the day I was planning to ask Holly Lawson to go to the dance with me. It is well known that you don't ask a girl to the dance without a serious **plan** to make sure she says yes.

Who's Holly Lawson? Only the most *beautiful* girl in our school. She is tall, slim, and has long blond hair that somehow manages to stay perfectly smooth and silky no matter what she is doing, or what the weather's like. I think it might be magic. *Girl* magic. My hair springs around on my head, making me look like a mad professor if I even breathe in the wrong direction.

It's not just me who thinks she is beautiful. Someone wrote: 'Who is the most beautiful girl in school?' in permanent marker in the boy's bathrooms outside the geography classes and within a few days, 'Holly Lawson' was written around it in a bunch of other pens by hundreds of different people! (Someone also wrote 'Jennifer Hunds' in small, neat handwriting near the bottom, but everyone knows that was written by Kyle Williams who has had a crush on her since Kindergarten, so that doesn't count.)

Everyone who was *anyone* wanted to ask Holly to the dance. Luckily, no one could because she is *my* girlfriend. Still, I wanted to be extra sure she would say yes, so I came up with the **plan**. I even wrote it down on a piece of paper so I wouldn't forget. This is what it said:

1.   Wait until Holly was putting stuff in her locker. It's on the ground floor right on the end.

2.   Put on 'cool guy' shades and jacket (which never fail with the ladies because I look so awesome in them).

3.   Lean against the wall, smile, put on my cool guy voice and say: "Hey Holly, you're my girlfriend and you're really pretty and stuff. We should totally go to the dance and stuff. For real."

Tom helped me come up with what to say. He just *knows* how to talk to girls. It's like a sixth sense or something. Needless to say, the plan was pretty much perfect. Tom suggested I bring flowers or something as well, but I was saving up for a new game so I couldn't afford it. Anyway, no girl (even one as hot as Holly) could resist the **plan**!

There was one slight hitch, though. In the morning I was running late and I left my 'cool guy' shades on my bed at home. Tom said that it didn't matter so much because Holly was already my girlfriend and knew how awesome I was.

That's why Tom is my best friend. He knows his stuff.

By the time we reached the lockers, we were breathing heavily and had to lean against the wall, but I could see Holly sorting out her stuff. We still had time.

"Go… get 'em… tiger…" Tom said between breaths.

I put a hand on his shoulder, leaning against him and said: "Thanks… buddy…"

By the time I walked over to Holly, I had caught my breath. I leaned against the locker next to her and cleared my throat.

Holly tucked her perfect hair behind her ear. "Hey Jack," she smiled. "What's up?"

I prepared myself mentally and put the **plan** into action:

"Hey Holly, you're my - Dad!"

Her locker door slowly closed and she looked at me with confused, brown eyes. "Excuse me?" she asked.

As I said. Disaster.

I should explain.

Just as I was about to say the smoothest line in the history of dance invitations, who should walk down the corridor in the opposite direction? My dad.

If you're wondering why my dad would casually be strolling around the halls of my school, it's because he works here. Yeah, I know. I'm the child of a teacher. He actually teaches the other 7th-grade class. Not the one I am in, thankfully.

Having your dad work at your school is bad and good. It's bad because it's your *dad* at *school.* He learns about EVERYTHING. Every mistake, every time I am told off, every breath I take, he learns about. It's horrible.

"Did you just call me your *dad?*" Holly asked, frowning.

"No, no," I began. "I just… you see… a **plan** and… well…" I didn't do a very good job at explaining myself.

"Jack Stevenson," my dad's voice boomed down the corridor. "What aren't you at *football practice?*"

Everyone in the corridor turned to look at me. My face felt like it was on fire. I tried to rapidly back away, but Dad managed to close the distance between us in record time. "I was just going!" I squeaked in a tiny voice, hoping the floor would swallow me up there and then.

Holly let out a small giggle. That's when I noticed I had been *leaning on some gum*! It had stuck itself to my t-shirt and now clung to me like an unbreakable spider web!

I felt sick. It was *disgusting!* The **plan** had failed and it was *all Dad's fault!*

Football Practice

Dad escorted me to the changing rooms. It was a walk of shame and everyone knew it. Holly offered a small wave as I walked past and I hung my head. I couldn't look anyone in the eye.

Tom had very smartly disappeared off to football practice as soon as he saw Dad coming. He was lucky.

Dad, on the other hand, didn't notice that he was ruining my life. He gave me the same old speech:

"You need to take *responsibility* for your actions, Jack."

"You're almost an adult, Jack. You need to take charge of your life."

"You're letting the *team down*, Jack."

Blah, blah, blah. Seriously, I could recite it in my sleep. Every time I tried to say something to try and explain what I was doing, he would raise his finger to his lips and shake his head until I stopped talking. He wouldn't listen to anything I was saying!

He left me in the changing room. I was glad to finally be rid of him as I put on my football kit and headed out onto the field, only to find out it got *worse*.

Who was there, waiting with the coach and the rest of my team? You guessed it. My dad. He was deep in conversation with Coach as I slowly walked towards them. I managed to glance over at Tom, who shook his head with wide eyes as if to say *Run. They're talking about you!*

I was about to do just that when Coach saw me and gave me **THE LOOK**. Coach is a chubby man, with no hair and a baseball cap permanently attached to his head. Tom once joked that he looked like a big baby. He is anything but that! When he uses **THE LOOK** you know you are in trouble. His forehead creases down into a tight 'V' shape and his lips are pressed so tight together they turn white and almost disappear.

"Stevenson!" He barked in a voice which made me flinch. "You're late!"

"I am, but…" I began to defend myself.

"No excuses," Dad said, shaking his head. "Coach and I have decided that the best thing for you to do now is to apologize to your team."

"Exactly!" Coach shouted. "Get apologizing Stevenson! Show me you *mean* it, and then 20 laps of the field!"

It was awful. I had to stand in front of my team as they sniggered and laughed at me, and say:

"I am very sorry for being late. I have let the team down and it will never happen again."

I might as well have committed social suicide right there. Even Tom was giggling by the end of it. He tried to fight it, but I saw his cheeks tighten as he fought not to smile. My dad, however, nodded slowly as I did it, pointing towards the team whenever I looked angrily at him.

When you are running around the football field, somehow it seems a *lot* larger than before. As I began my punishment and my friends went back to playing football, I was *furious*. If my dad hadn't been here, everything would have been fine. The **plan** would have been a success, I would have been playing football with them, and I wouldn't have to explain to Holly why I called her my dad. Instead, I was getting all hot and sweaty; my legs burned from running around the rectangular field with the cheerleaders laughing and jeering every time I went passed them. With every step, the same thoughts looped through my mind:

Why couldn't my dad see that he was *ruining* my life? He doesn't understand that what he does is the *worst*. I wished somehow he could see it from *my perspective*. Maybe then he wouldn't be so smug.

Little did I know, I'd later regret I had even thought that.

After Practice

When practice had finished, I was still angry. I had missed half of it running around the field, and by the time I managed to get back in, my head was all over the place and I played terribly. Coach yelled at me for 'not giving it my all' and it just made things worse.

"Huddle up!" Coach called us all together in a group once he had finished yelling at me. "Now kids, I've got a little announcement."

Tom glanced at me to see if I knew anything. I shrugged. I didn't have a clue.

"I've heard that some of you have a little Math exam tomorrow," Coach said, looking directly at me. "And I've decided that if you *don't* pass the exam, you aren't going to be playing the first match in a few weeks."

The team broke out into protests and shouts, mine being the loudest, but Coach raised his hands, silencing us all. "Don't think being good at sport means you can slack off in class. That's all, let's get changed." He blew his whistle and waved us back to the changing room.

Tom moved next to me as we ran. "I bet Mr. Thomas spoke to your dad about today and your dad spoke to *Coach*. This is their doing."

My jaw tightened. Tom was right. This had my dad's and Mr. Thomas's evil smeared all over it. They were actively trying to make my life *hell*.

I tried not to think about it as I got changed, but failed. My dad had ruined my chance with Holly, and now he wanted to ruin my chances to get on the team as well? What was wrong with him? Why did he want me to be unhappy?

To make things worse, I still had to wait for him to finish work at school. After I said goodbye to Tom, I decided to head back to the field and kick field goals until Dad was done. I had managed to catch a glimpse of a new technique taught by Coach during the practice, every time I passed them when running laps, so I decided to have a go at that while I waited.

I dropped the ball and kicked it as hard as I could. It flew off, a bit off target from where it was supposed to go, but it felt good. The thump of my foot against the ball was great. I imagined it was my dad's head the next time I kicked it and laughed as the imaginary head went screaming into the air in front of me.

Sure, I probably looked a bit *crazy*, but it was worth it.

Soon, I was really getting the hang of the new technique. I was sure that if I kept it up, I would go pro in no time. Not only would that be amazing, but it would also mean I wouldn't have to do any more Math lessons or stupid Math exams.

After a few more kicks, I was sure that I was doing the *best* I had ever done (no one was there to see…typical). I put on my 'Football Jam mix' on my phone and listened to my favorite band: The Spiky Monkeys. Every kick was perfect and with the band rocking out in my headphones I was beginning to feel a lot better.

Then, of course, it started to rain.

As I looked up at the sky, now dark and gray, I remembered that it was incredibly sunny when we had started practice. But now, the sun had disappeared and thick, dark clouds had appeared in its place. It was the perfect end to the perfect day. Typical.

"Jack!" A hand placed on my shoulder made me jump. I turned to find Dad standing next to me and pulled out my headphones. "Come on, time to go home."

Something inside me clenched in anger and I refused to move. "I'm going to do one more kick," I said, picking up the ball again and walking back up the field.

"Excuse me?" Dad said, following me. "I said we have to go, come on."

"I'm going to do one more kick!" I snapped back, all the anger of the day coming back. "I missed most of practice after all!"

Dad stopped, stunned for a second, his mouth opening and closing like a fish. "Don't kick that ball, Jack," he said quietly. "I'm warning you."

He's warning me, a little voice in my head taunted. I looked him dead in the eye and raised my foot.

"Don't do it, Jack," he said again.

I dropped the ball and kicked it with all my strength. *That'll show him*, I thought. The ball flew off down the field.

Dad's face went all red like he was about to yell at me, but it was at that exact moment that the rain *really* started to pour down. There was even a loud crack of thunder across the sky.

We both looked upward. The sky was black now, apart from the occasional flash of lightning. The wind whipped around us in a howling gale and I could barely hear my dad as he shouted, "Jack! We need to get to the car!" I wanted to kick the ball again, but with the weather as it was, I knew it wasn't going to happen. I shook my head and walked towards him.

"Don't think I've forgotten about that kick," Dad yelled at me through the rain.

"Don't think *I've* forgotten about how you're *ruining my life!*" I screamed back. The thunder even crashed right after I said it (it was pretty awesome).

We were both running now towards the parking lot where Dad had left his car. Dad pointed at the gate on the other side of the field. "If we can just…"

CRASH.

Whatever Dad was *going* to say was lost as lightning struck the end zone of the field in front of us! On the ground was a little scorch mark where it had struck. Dad and I both stopped and stared at it.

"Run!" Dad shouted. "Over the fence!"

He pointed towards a short cut. The parking lot was just over a small metallic fence. We could climb over it in no time and cut the distance in half. I didn't argue. That could be done later. We both set off at a sprint in that direction.

CRASH.

Lightning struck again, right where my Dad had been standing previously. It was like it was *trying* to strike us!

That persuaded me to run a little faster.

We both reached the fence at the same time. All we had to do was hop over it. We both grabbed it to leap over it and-

CRASH.

That's when the world went black.

After the Storm

When I opened my eyes, I was staring at the gray sky above me. The inside of my mouth tasted like Dad's 'Chicken Surprise' (the surprise is that it tastes like old fish wrapped in foil and that he *still* tries to make it every few weeks) and my head was spinning. The lightning, however, seemed to have stopped. The weather had gone back to a light rain.

I sat up and saw that I was on the other side of the fence. Had I been struck by *lightning?* Whatever had happened, I had made it to the other side successfully. I decided to get to the car as quickly as possible, in case the weather decided to change again. Slowly, I pushed myself to my feet. My legs wobbled and shook with each step, but I managed to convince my feet to work together long enough to get to Dad's green Rust Bucket (that's what I call his car. It's a piece of junk). I opened the passenger door and went to sit down.

CLONK.

My head struck the door frame. Pain spiked through my skull and shook my teeth.

Ow, I thought, rubbing my head. I *really* didn't need that right now. I stared angrily at the Rust Bucket, blaming it for my pain. Something was wrong though. The Rust Bucket was *smaller* than I remembered. I frowned and got inside, still rubbing my head.

The other door to the car opened and closed as Dad got in. We both sat in silence for a while.

"What happened?" Dad asked.

Except… it *wasn't* my dad's voice. His voice was high and strange like he had been sucking on helium balloons. I turned, shocked and not at all prepared for what I saw. Sitting in the driver seat of the car was a young boy, with a scraggly mess of hair on his head, wearing my school's football kit. It wasn't my dad. It was *me!*

"What…" I began, my hands shaking when I realized something else horrifying. *My voice was low.* It was like my voice was a truck's engine. I looked in the rearview mirror to see what was wrong and what stared back at me was horrifying. I was *old*. My hair was neatly combed into place. I was wearing a strange shirt that had all the buttons done up tightly. I was in *my dad's body!*

Unsurprisingly, I freaked out. I tried to back out of the car quickly, wanting to get some fresh air, but only managed to hit my head on the roof again as I pushed away.

CLONK.

"Ow!" I hissed again in my very *very* deep voice.

Dad, wearing my face, looked at me with horror and I stared at him.

Now, in situations like this, you should probably stay calm. That's what they tell you to do at school when it's an emergency, and this was definitely an emergency.

So I decided to say: "Oh dear, we seem to have swapped bodies, whatever shall we do, Dad?"

The only problem is it sounded like this:

"ARRRRRRGGGGGHHHHHHHHHH!"

When he recalls the story later, he says that *he* said: "Keep calm, Jack, everything will be alright." However, to me, it sounded a lot like:

"ARRRRRRGGGGGHHHHHHHHHHHHH!"

We continued to scream and look at each other and scream and look at ourselves and scream for a while. Right until our throats pretty much gave up on screaming and we had to sit in the car in a dull silence.

When we had both finally calmed down, I turned to my dad again.

"How…but…why…?" Words were hard. My brain felt like porridge and I still felt uncomfortable speaking in my dad's voice.

Dad rested his hands on the steering wheel of the car, slowly turned to me with wide eyes, and said in a very quiet voice: "You need to drive us home."

We both looked down. Dad wiggled his new legs in the direction of the car pedals. They were too short.

"Oh," I said. *Oh no*, I thought.

A Driving Lesson

I had always hoped that my first time driving a car would be when I was sixteen, and I would be a master at it right away. After all, whenever I played racing games against Tom, he *always* lost because I was so good. So driving a car in real life shouldn't be so different, right? Just push the buttons (or pedals) and it goes forward.

Wrong.

After we had swapped seats, Dad spent what felt like an hour explaining to me the different mirrors, the pedals, how to break properly, how I needed to be *aware* at all times and lots of other things like that.

I just sat with my hands resting on the steering wheel in front of me and stared out at the parking lot, terrified to move.

"Are you ready?" he finally asked. "We are going to take it *slow* around the parking lot, OK?"

My mouth was dry. Really, really dry. I nodded.

Slowly, I turned the key in the ignition. The engine of the car rumbled to life. I felt it vibrate the seat beneath me. Had it *always* been like this? The car suddenly felt like a large, hulking, uncontrollable monster.

"Nice and slow now," Dad repeated.

I took a deep breath. "It's OK, Dad," I said. "I think I understand the-"

I put my foot on the accelerator and the Rust Bucket jolted forward, A LOT faster than I expected.

"SLOW SLOW SLOW!" My dad shouted and I slammed my foot onto the brake pedal. We were thrown forward in our seats as the Rust Bucket came to an abrupt halt.

I turned to Dad. He scowled at me. I grinned back. "Easy as pie," I said weakly. Dad didn't seem to agree. I wasn't sure I did either. My heart was pounding loudly in my ears.

I had always dreamed of turning up to school in a red Ferrari and making all my friends jealous, (ultimately, of course, they would all want to hang out and go on road trips with me). Now I could see that dream melting away in front of my eyes, slowly being replaced by one single emotion: terror. Why did they make it look so easy on TV?

We started again slowly. I gently pressed my foot onto the pedal and the Rust Bucket rumbled to life, slowly creeping forward. After doing a few laps around the parking lot, Dad took a deep breath and said: "OK, let's guide her out onto the road. Slowly."

I nodded. *I can do this* I thought to myself. *I am Jack Stevenson and I can-*

HONK.

I slammed my foot onto the brake again.

A red car accelerated past us. I tried not to focus too hard on how I had nearly gotten us both killed. Dad gripped onto the door with white knuckles. "It's OK," he said, over and over again. "It's all a dream. I'm going to wake up in a second. Everything will be fine."

"Dad?" I asked, ignoring him. "Should I go now?"

He slowly opened one eye and looked at the traffic around us. "OK," he said. "Slowly now."

'Slowly' became the word of the trip. Every time I started to go slightly faster than a snail's pace, my dad would scream at me and I would slam my foot on the brake, throwing us forward.

I always used to wonder why my dad got angry at other drivers when he was in the car, but after five minutes on the road, I began to realize why.

HONK. HONK. HOOOOOOOOOOOOOOONK.

Every other driver honked their horns. Red, angry faces glared at us through windows as they sped past or crept behind us.

Everyone seemed to be in an extreme hurry to get somewhere and they were very angry at me for not going fast enough. When I finally turned off the main road into our quieter street, I felt the pressure in the car go down as we both let out a long breath.

"Well done," Dad said.

"Thanks," I grinned.

"I was talking to myself," Dad replied, wiping sweat off his brow. "From now on, we are *walking* everywhere!"

I would have argued, but I was too tired. I pulled the car slooooooowly into our drive and turned off the engine. "It wasn't that bad…" I mumbled as Dad got out of the car.

I sat silent and alone in the car and closed my eyes, hoping and praying for everything to return to normal.

I wasn't that lucky.

The Next Day

When I woke up the next morning, my prayers hadn't been answered. The only thing that was different was that I had a pain in my neck from sleeping in my bed, which was suddenly far too small for me, and ice cold feet because they had been sticking out from under my comforter.

I sat up in bed and groaned a loud, deep groan. Is this what it was like to be an adult all the time? I never wanted to grow up. It was so tiring. I looked down at my new legs and saw how they were so big and lanky, covered in dark, black hairs. They felt all itchy and strange and on closer inspection in a mirror, my face was sprouting hairs as well. Everything felt *wrong*. No wonder Dad was so weird.

With a grimace, I stepped over my clothes on the floor and opened my bedroom door.

"Agh!" I shouted. Stood right outside was Dad, a sleepy look in his eyes, or *my* eyes. He yawned loudly and held up the bottom half of his blue pajamas with his free hand. They were *way* too big for him in my body and were constantly trying to fall down.

"We haven't changed back," he said. "This isn't good."

"You're telling me. How do you live like this?" I asked, scratching my new head.

Dad stared at me for a while, blinking the tiredness out his eyes. He had never been a morning person. I could see his brain slowly working through all possible ideas to help us out of the situation. His brain finally gave up and he simply said:

"Breakfast."

I nodded. At least we could agree on that.

It turned out that even simple things like breakfast were now difficult. Dad kept dropping things, unsure how to use his smaller hands properly. I had to reach into the higher cupboards to help him get the bowls out and when he tried to pour the milk on the cereal, he fumbled and dropped it, spilling it everywhere.

As we both stared at the milky mess on the floor, he sighed loudly. "Great," he mumbled. "This isn't going work." He then decided two things:

> 1.   I couldn't go into his work today. After all, I didn't know how to teach a class.
> 2.   If this body swap hadn't sorted itself out by the end of the day, we were going to the doctors to see if they could help.

As much as I *hated* the doctors, the thought of being stuck in my dad's body for much longer was worse, so I agreed. It was the smell that I really hated, so I decided I could just hold my nose for the time I was there.

"I could probably teach a class," I said, stirring my bowl of cereal with my spoon. "How hard could it be?"

Dad didn't stop mopping up the milk on the floor. "No," he said without looking up.

"Just a little class, don't know if I don't try, right?" I grinned.

Dad stopped and looked me dead in the eye. "No, Jack," he said (it would have sounded a lot more serious in his voice, I'm sure). "I can't have you acting unprofessionally in front of my students."

"I *won't* be unprofessional!"

Dad looked at me as if to say: *Really?*

Yes, OK, I probably would have been a *little* unprofessional, but I had a reason! There's a boy in his class, Tommy Wilkins, who is a *super* nerd. He thinks he is smarter than everyone, even some of the teachers, and likes to rub your nose in it. Honestly, he's just really annoying.

I just wanted to see how he would cope with a trip to the Principal's office to ruin his 'perfect student' rep....

"You're not going in, end of story."

I shrugged. I wasn't going to complain about a day off. "Wait," I said. "What are *you* doing?"

Dad dropped the sponge he was using in the sink. "I'm staying off too."

I wasn't going to say anything when something clicked in my head. The Math exam! If I didn't manage to pass it, I wouldn't be allowed to play in the first match and then we wouldn't win and…a master plan suddenly formed in my head. A masterfully crafted master plan.

Dad was about to leave the room when I squeaked: "But what about my *grades*?"

Dad paused. I had him like a fish on a line. "I mean," I continued, "I have a test today. An *important* one. We shouldn't let a little thing like swapping bodies affect my studies, should we? Not if I want me to go to a good college." I let that one dangle in the air for a while. "I mean, you could leave right after you've done it, pick up my homework and make sure I don't miss anything."

He turned back to me with an odd smile on his face. "I'm proud of you, Jack, for being so mature and thinking about your studies. You're right." He nodded to himself. "I'll go in and pretend to be you. Shouldn't be too hard." And with that, he turned and left the room.

"*Shouldn't be too hard*!" I shouted after him. "What does that mean?"

It was a few minutes later when he emerged from my room that I found out what he meant. Maybe my masterfully crafted plan wasn't as great as I thought it was.

He was wearing the worst outfit I had ever been forced to wear for my aunt's fortieth birthday last year: a tight white shirt with an itchy, dark blue sweater vest over the top, a bow tie (where did he even *find* that?) and black, smart trousers. He stood in my doorway, smoothing down the vest and smiling to himself. "Very nice," he said. "Smart and respectful."

"No!" I shouted. "You aren't wearing that!"

He looked offended. "Why not? I think I look pretty snazzy."

"Snazzy? *Snazzy?*" I felt like my head was about to explode. "You can't wear that to *school*! I'll be the laughing stock of the whole city!"

Dad shrugged. "I think it's alright. When I was at school…."

"Dinosaurs ruled the earth and didn't have any fashion sense," I interrupted him. "Look, let me sort out what you're going to wear." I pushed past him into the room and started rummaging through my wardrobe.

"You need to tidy your room," he mumbled, standing behind me.

I snapped my head around. "Not now," I snarled. Dad just chuckled.

As I sorted through my wardrobe for a decent pair of jeans and a clean t-shirt, Dad disappeared from the room. By the time he came back, I had an outfit laying down on the bed ready for him.

"That's what you're wearing today," I announced.

"Maybe," he said and then held out a small piece of paper. "If you do this."

I took the paper. "What is it?"

"A script. I need you to call in sick for me. With *my* voice," Dad grinned. I recognized the grin on his face.

On *my* face. I thought for the whole time I was playing him, but he had played *me* as well. I sighed and looked at the script in my hand. This is what it said:

Call Mrs. Jade the receptionist 'Beverly' because that is her name.

READ THIS WHEN SHE ANSWERS THE PHONE:

Hello, Beverly. It's David Stevenson here. I'm afraid that I am not going to make it in today as I am very sick. I am very sorry for the inconvenience I have caused. I hope you can find an adequate supply teacher. Thank you very much. Goodbye.

If she tries to say anything more <u>say you are too ill and hang up!</u>

The last line was underlined. He obviously didn't want me speaking too much. I glanced at Dad. "You want me to read this?"

"Word for word." He handed me his mobile, the number of the school already typed into it. "Just do it now and quickly."

I rolled my eyes as he waved the bow tie at me again. I made a secret promise to *burn* the bow tie when this was all over and pressed the call button on the phone. It began to ring. Nerves shot down my body with each ring. I had to sound convincing.

"Hello?" Mrs. Jade's soft voice spoke on the other end of the line.

"Hello, Mrs., ah, Beverly… It's Ja- er David Stevenson here." I could feel my palms getting incredibly sweaty. Dad shook his head slowly as he watched me. I decided to get it done as soon as possible. "I'mafraidthatIamnotgoingtomakeitinasIamsick." The words spilled out of me as nerves gripped my throat.

"Pardon?" Mrs. Jade said. I silently kicked myself and tried to get some oxygen into my lungs.

I started again: "Hello, *Beverly*. It. Is. David. Stevenson. Here. I'm. Afraid. That. I am. Not. Going. To. Make. It. In. Today. As. I am. Very. Sick."

"Oh, David!" Mrs. Jade replied. "I'm very sorry to hear that. What's wrong?"

I blinked. There wasn't an answer to that on the script. Dad stared at me hopefully. I decided to plow onward. "I'm very sorry for the in… incon… in…" I stared at my Dad's handwriting. What was the word?

Dad started waving his hands and mouthing: HANG UP! HANG UP!

I gave up. "Sorry, I'm too ill. Going to vomit! Byeeeeee! *blllleeeeuuuugh*" I hung up while making sick noises just to add to the effect and then smiled sweetly at my dad.

"Better than nothing," he sighed, snatching the clothes off the bed.

I felt like I had won that round.

The Day Off

Dad stood by the open door and watched the school bus drive slowly down the street. He looked like he had just eaten a rotten egg as he watched the ancient metal beast chug slowly towards us, yellow paint scratched off after years of use.

"I have to go in that…deathtrap with all those kids?" he groaned.

I nodded, not trying to hide my smile at all. "Don't sit too near the front, or people will throw stuff at you. Oh, and don't sit too near the back either. The *weird* kids sit there." Dad blinked at me, his brain clearly not processing the information I was giving him. "They will probably try to bite you," I added, stirring him up further, just for good measure.

I handed him a letter he had typed out so he could hand it in at the office, allowing him to leave early. "You can sign this, I'm sure."

He took it reluctantly and shook his head. "I can't believe I'm doing this."

"Oh and don't forget, you have to *walk* home this afternoon."

"Walk?" His eyes widened. "But its *miles* away!"

I remembered the first time I had to walk home from school. It was a very long way and my legs were killing me by the end of it. My smile widened even further. "Welcome to my world!" I winked and then closed the door before he could protest. I was home alone and I could do what I wanted!

What followed was, in short, the best day *ever.* Sure, I was stuck in my dad's body and sure, I had to wear his boring clothes (all of which smelled like that odd 'man perfume' that Dad is so fond of wearing. It smells like something you would use to clean a toilet), but I got to do whatever I wanted. I decided to make the most of my free time and wrote out a list:

Awesome things to do for my awesome day:

    1.   Eat Candy

    2.   Play Minecraft

    3.   Play Skylanders

    4.   Eat MORE Candy

    5.   Listen to SUPER LOUD MUSIC

    6.   Minecraft it up again. (Or Call of Duty, or both)

    7.   Junk Food/Candy

    8.   Maybe a nap?

    9.   Play guitar and drums REALLY LOUDLY

    10.   Junk food again. Or Candy. Maybe both.

I'm not going to lie: I made it through most of my list. It was a really productive day! Although, by the time I reached number seven, I had eaten so many bars of chocolate (Dad stored them in the cupboard I couldn't reach, but now I *could*!) that I was starting to feel a little sick and decided to maybe give eating a little bit of a break. I managed to build so much on Minecraft, it was insane. At first, Dad's big floppy fingers made holding the controller weird and I kept dropping it. However, after a few hours, I got the hang of them. I would even go as far as saying that I was *better than before!* I also managed to set up a little fort on the couch made from pillows and blankets (so I could defend the house in case anyone decided to try and get in).

The only person who tried was the postman, but he just pushed letters through the door and walked away again. If he *had* tried to get in, though, I was ready for him!

I even started to think that maybe this body swapping thing wasn't the end of the world. I decided I could probably cope with it for a little while.

I didn't notice Dad coming home in the afternoon. I was too busy fighting zombies. I only realized he was back when he slumped down on the sofa beside me, dropping my school bag to the floor. He sighed loudly and closed his eyes. I didn't bother to pause the game or even look his way. I just grinned and said: "Fun day?"

I could feel his scowl burning into the side of my face as I continued to shoot zombies.

"The school bus was... stressful," he said. "I see you've gotten comfy while I've been away."

46

I smiled even wider. "Well you know, I kept myself busy," I joked. "Didn't want to get bored."

"Yes, that would be terrible," he replied sarcastically, picking up a handful of candy bar wrappers from the floor. He stood up and turned on the computer in the corner of the room, the screen glowing as it sprang to life.

"What are you doing?" I asked, spraying the handful of chips I had just shoved in my mouth everywhere and finally prizing my attention away from my own screen.

"I'm seeing if the Internet has any answers to our little... *problem*." He waved his hands between us. "It is a powerful tool, after all."

Wow, leave it to my dad to make even the Internet sound boring. 'A powerful tool'. *Really?* It wasn't a terrible idea. My character screamed as zombies began to eat him alive. I threw my controller on the floor and wandered over to my Dad, to see if his search was going to produce any results.

Dad typed (incredibly slowly, with one finger) the words "Body Swapping" into the search engine. He scrolled down the screen and we examined the results.

Here are a few:

WOMAN CLAIMS TO HAVE SWAPPED BODIES WITH CAT – SAYS SHE COUGHED UP HAIRBALLS FOR A WEEK.

SALLY'S FASHION BLOG – 15 FASHION TIPS TO SWAP YOUR BODY WITH THE BODY OF YOUR FAVORITE CELEB

SWAP YOUR FAT BODY WITH A FIT BODY IN THREE DAYS WITH THIS SIMPLE TRICK!

Dad hovered over the last one for slightly too long. I placed a hand on his shoulder and shook my head.

"It's a scam, Dad," I said. "Just let it go."

Dad rolled his eyes. "Obviously. I am well aware of that." Slowly he moved the mouse upward and bookmarked the page. He never listens to me. "Just in case," he mumbled as I shook my head disapprovingly. He clicked on the next page and shook his head. "This page just had a bunch of links about an actress called Lindsey Lohan. What's she got to do with this?"

I shrugged. "Not a clue. Have you tried 'Lightning strike'? Or 'Mind swap'? Or maybe a search which involves…."

Dad stood up. "I can't stand technology. You do it." He walked to the door of the room. "I'm going to start making dinner."

My stomach ached at the thought of more food after the amount I had stuffed myself with, but I didn't want Dad to know that, so I replied: "Good plan. I'll stay here."

What followed was an Internet search which went on for *hours*. OK, it was closer to twenty minutes, but by the end, I was horrifically bored and no more enlightened. I did, however, find out that the chances of being struck by lightning were 300,000 to 1 which meant that Dad and I were… lucky? I guess? I informed him of what I had found when he came back into the room with plates of sandwiches.

"Oh," he said. "That's interesting. But what if-" he was interrupted by the house phone starting to ring. He looked at me and I looked at him. We both looked at the phone. "Answer it!" he whispered to me, pointing at the phone.

My eyes widened. "You answer it!" I whispered back. I wasn't going to answer the phone. What if it was one of Dad's friends? How was I supposed to talk to them?

"What if it's someone from work?" Dad said frantically.

"Tell them I am ill… or you're ill… or… just answer it!"

Dad slowly edged towards the phone like it was an atom bomb and picked up the receiver. "Hello?" he said quietly. There was a pause. A long pause. It felt like forever before he finally said. "Oh, hello Tom!" I breathed a sigh of relief. "I suppose you want to talk to Jack…" I stopped breathing again.

No Dad, you're Jack now! Remember?!

Dad suddenly realized what he had said and backtracked poorly. "I mean *I'm* Jack! Of course, I am! You want to talk to me. Your best friend. Jack. Who is me."

He looked at me apologetically as Tom probably called him crazy on the other end of the line. My hands clenched tightly on the arms of the seat. Not being part of the conversation was torture. What was Tom saying? By the way, Dad frowned, it wasn't something good. "OH," Dad suddenly said very loudly, as if I couldn't hear, "TONIGHT. THE DINNER PLANS WE MADE. OF COURSE. AT YOUR HOUSE."

Fear clamped down on my stomach, threatening to bring back the day's worth of junk food. In all the excitement of body swapping, we had completely forgotten about the dinner plans we had made for this evening!

It may sound a bit weird, but my dad and Tom's mom, Sarah, had been sort of thinking about dating for a while. Dad had sat down and asked me if it was OK and at first, I was horrified by the idea. Dad had suggested that maybe if we all sat down to dinner one evening, then maybe I would have a change of heart. I wasn't *completely* convinced, but when Dad said that I could spend the evening gaming with Tom while he and Sarah talked, I didn't say no. I mean, what was the worst that could happen?

Obviously, I never expected to be stuck in my dad's body! The thought of having to date Tom's mom made those candy bars start to rise into my throat again.

"No, no, sorry, we can't do tonight," Dad said. I let out a sigh of relief. "Why? Oh, Dad's far too ill. Yeah, he's been vomiting all day, it's been really super gross...er...dude."

Dude? I shook my head. No one says 'dude' anymore! My dad was stuck in the past.

Dad laughed uncomfortably. "Yeah I do sound like my dad, don't I? He is such a...dork. I mean...yeah, you know."

It was painful watching him pretend to be me. I started gesturing to him to put the phone down. He nodded.

"Alright, byeeeeeeee." Dad put the phone down and shook his head. "That was awful."

"You're telling me," I sighed. "We need to get back into our own bodies as soon as possible." Dad nodded in agreement.

"I'm booking a doctor's appointment for tonight," he said.

Back on the Road

"I really didn't want to have to do this again for another few years," I groaned as I sat in the driver's seat of the car.

Dad nodded, doing up his seatbelt and testing it a few times. "Don't think that I *want* you to do it, but we need to get to the doctor's appointment and we will be late if we don't drive." He took a deep breath. "Don't worry, this time, we are going to take it nice and slow, no panicking, just a calm and easy drive."

I looked at him. He was an awful liar.

"Just remember," he said sternly. "Listen to what I say!"

"Do you mean when you say things like: 'Oh God, I'm too young to die?'"

"Yes, well...no," Dad mumbled, getting flustered. "Just take it slow. Slooooow." He spoke to me as if I was a kindergartener.

I shook my head and turned the key. The Rust Bucket rumbled to life. "Ugh, not again," I whispered and gently put my foot down on the accelerator.

Every time we went over ten miles per hour, Dad let out a small squeak and told me to slow down. We crept along the road, people honking their horns and overtaking us whenever possible. I tried to hide my face whenever they passed, but it would just make Dad scream more if I 'wasn't paying attention to the road'. It was so *embarrassing.*

"Careful!" Dad shouted again for what felt like the 100th time.

"Why? Worried we are going to lose control of the car?" I moaned back wiggling the steering wheel back and forth, making the car shake and wiggle.

"No, I mean that…."

The siren from behind us interrupted Dad before he could finish his sentence.

"The police are right behind us," Dad sighed. He closed his eyes and leaned back in his chair. "This is going to end badly. I can tell."

"Thanks for the vote of confidence," I mumbled. Although to be honest, I didn't have confidence in me either! My hands were shaking as I pulled onto the side of the road. I was far too young to go to jail, even if I didn't look it. I briefly considered driving away, but Dad shook his head.

"It'll be fine," he whispered, handing me his license from the front of the car. I didn't believe it. He didn't believe it.

We both sat and waited for the police officer to pull up behind us and get out of his car. He seemed to do everything in slow motion, getting out of his car, standing and staring for a few seconds and then walking towards us at a snail's pace.

"Why is he taking so long?" I squeaked

"To make you panic. You need to *stay calm*, Jack. Just do what he says and everything will be alright." The way Dad spoke to me, his voice wobbling like mine, made me realize that he was as freaked out as I was. I had no idea what to expect.

TAP. TAP. TAP. The cop finally reached the window beside me and tapped his knuckle against my window. That's when I noticed how much my hands were sweating. "Open the window!" Dad said, poking me in the arm.

"Oh, right." I fumbled around with the window control until finally, the glass pane slid downward with a quiet buzz. The cop watched from behind big, round sunglasses. He didn't look anything like the fat, donut loving cops I was used to seeing on TV. This cop was built like a brick wall, with puffed out cheeks, square jaw and a mouth that looked like it had never learned how to smile.

"Hello," I croaked. "How can I help you?" I was already failing to stay calm. I just hoped it wasn't *too* obvious.

"License and registration please, sir," the officer said in a stern monotone voice that suggested he could break me in half like a twig and then chew up the remains. I glanced over at Dad, who just pointed frantically at the police officer again. I handed him the license that Dad had given to me, hoping that my hand sweat wouldn't be all over the card. The officer took it and stood for a while writing something down in a tiny notepad he produced from his pocket.

He wrote.

He wrote some more.

He glanced at the card.

He wrote something more.

I glanced at the clock in the car. This was worse than Math.

OK, maybe that was going a bit far.

Finally, he handed the card back and said: "Do you realize how fast you were going, sir?"

I thought about it. Was he joking? He didn't *seem* to be joking. I wasn't sure he could do any emotions other than terrifying or angry. "I definitely wasn't going over the speed limit!" I said with a (hopefully) cheerful smile. I mean, that's what people are arrested for right? Going too fast?

The police officer stared at me for a second. I could hear the cogs whirring in his head. "No sir, you most certainly were not."

Good, I thought to myself. *I guess he'll just let us go then. Maybe he just wanted a chat.*

We weren't that lucky. Instead, the officer lowered his sunglasses, revealing terrifying light blue eyes, and asked: "Have you been drinking sir?"

Before I could respond, Dad pushed forward and leaned over me. "Of *course* he hasn't!" he said in an irritable voice. "He is *far* too young to be doing anything like that!"

The officer opened his mouth and then closed it again. He looked incredibly confused. I wasn't surprised. I dragged Dad backward and tried to smile again.

"He means…er…" I racked my brains to come up with something that didn't sound completely insane. "That the night is young! It's too early to drink now, so I'm not drinking yet. Not that I plan to drink later. Of course not. Don't drink and drive." I smiled with too many teeth as the officer tried to get through the absolute madness that had just spewed out of my mouth.

"Right," he said. "Please step out of the car sir; I believe you are driving under the influence of alcohol."

"But I'm not!" I tried to argue.

"Do I have to *remove* you from your vehicle, sir?" He took an aggressive step forward.

"No, no, no," I squeaked. "I'm getting out." I imagined being removed from the car would involve the cop squeezing the vehicle like a tube of toothpaste until I popped out. I opened the car door. My legs began to wobble like jelly and I tried to look confident and, more importantly, innocent.

As I did, the officer said: "No one drives *that* slow if they're not trying to hide something!"

I had to admit, the cop wasn't too far off. We were trying to hide something, just not what he thought.

"Er, *Dad*," Dad popped his head out of the car window. "Is everything alright?"

"Yes, this very nice police officer just thinks we were driving too slow, *son*." I shot Dad a look to suggest it was all his fault. He looked ashamed.

"Please return to your seat," the police officer said to Dad and then turned back to me. He produced a small device which looked like a box with a straw on the end. "This is a breathalyzer," he said. "I want you to breath into here," he pointed at the straw, "and *then* we'll see if the night is too young for drinking or not!"

I took the box and examined the straw, trying not to think how many other people had breathed into it. It looked like someone had even tried to chew on it as well. Closing my eyes, I put the straw in my mouth and blew into it. It tasted like soap. I kept blowing until the device beeped and the cop signaled I could take it out of my mouth. I spat on the ground as he took the device back and tried to wipe the taste away.

"That tasted awful!" I moaned, spitting again and again. "Do you ever clean that?"

The officer didn't bother to look up at me. "That is the taste of *justice*," he said, pressing a button on the device. It beeped again.

"Well, justice tastes *gross*," I said, grimacing. "What does the breathy thing say?"

After what felt like another horrifically long pause, the device beeped again. The officer didn't do a very good job at hiding his surprise. "Oh," he said. "Er... it seemed that you aren't as drunk as I thought you were."

"That *is* a surprise," I said, rolling my eyes. "I thought I was incredibly drunk."

The police officer raised his eyebrows. "Excuse me?"

"I was joking!" I squeaked.

"The police department does NOT have a sense of humor! If you are drunk and my device is malfunctioning, you are required to tell me RIGHT NOW!" He moved right up into my face until I could smell his sour, old coffee breath.

"No, no, no, no, no!" I stammered. "I'm not drunk! Not at all!"

He stared...and then moved away. "OK then," he said. "I'll let you off this time. But I'll be watching you."

"T…thank you!" I squeaked and hopped back into the car. I let out a long breath as I sat and stared out in front of us. "Is he gone?" I asked.

"Nope," Dad said. "He is just staring at us."

"Right," I said, deciding that getting as far away as possible from the police officer was a good idea. "I might drive a little faster this time if you don't mind."

Dad agreed. "But only a little bit," he added as I pulled away from the curb. I shook my head. When would he learn?

300,000 to 1

Even though we drove a little faster from that point, we were still *very* late for our doctor's appointment.

The doctor's office was located in a small building just on the edge of the city. We entered the small waiting room, both sweating and breathing heavily. Dad was the first to go up to the desk. "Sorry, we're late. We have an appointment under the name Stevenson."

The nurse behind the desk looked at Dad and then over to me. She took a long, slow breath and then pulled out some forms from a drawer under her desk. She handed them to Dad. "Have your dad fill out these forms, kid," she said, before turning back to her computer and clicking down the keys. Dad looked down at the forms and then waved me over; the only pen available in the office was on a small chain next to the nurse.

"You have to fill out these forms *Dad*," he said with a roll of the eyes. I went over and, with Dad telling me what to do, I filled out each box slowly, trying to keep my handwriting as 'adulty' and neat as possible, occasionally adding little flicks for effect. The nurse glanced over with a raised eyebrow as a young son told his dad what to do, but didn't seem too bothered by it overall. When we were finally done, I handed her the form and she shoved it back into her drawer without even bothering to read it.

She just thrust a finger at the waiting room chairs and said: "The doctor will call you when she's ready."

We sat down in the chairs and began to wait. An old man on the far side of the room coughed and wheezed and choked. A baby cried and exploded snot out of its nose with every scream, spraying anything that was too close. I shuffled closer to Dad. *This* is why I hate going to the doctors. We watched the old man disappear into a room when called. We watched the mother drag her crying baby into another room. We continued to wait.

"I could have driven even slower and been pulled over *again* at this rate," I joked to Dad. He didn't reply. He looked like a dark cloud had settled over his head.

"I can't believe they're making us wait this long."

"Well, I mean we were-" I was interrupted by a doctor appearing in the doorway. He looked a little like one of the teachers at school, with spiky brown hair that stuck out the sides and a large bald patch on top of his head. He glanced down at a clipboard in his hand and said:

"Stevenson?"

We looked around the waiting room. It was empty except for us and the *germs*.

"I guess that's you!" he said with a grin. "I'm Doctor Edwards. Follow me."

He led us down a tight corridor to a small room at the end. The further we went into the building, the more it smelled like disinfectant and illness. I tried not to breathe too deeply, in case something decided to leap into my mouth and infect me.

His office was surprisingly large. Certificates of different degrees covered the wall and he sat on the other side of the desk. Typing something into his computer, he turned back to us with the same smile as before.

"So, how can I help you?"

I was about to speak when Dad said: "We were struck by lightning."

Doctor Edwards blinked. He turned back to his computer as if to type something in, but his fingers hovered over the keyboard. He turned back to us. "Struck by lightning? Both of you?" he said, as if unsure of the words coming out of his mouth.

"Apparently there is a 300,000 to 1 chance of it happening," I chirped in. Dad gave me a look. I shrugged. "What? It's true. I read it on the Internet."

"Ok…er… *Where* did you get struck by lightning?" he asked

"On a football field," I answered.

"No, I meant on your body," he said again.

"Oh," I paused. Where did I get struck? That was a good question. I didn't hurt anywhere and I didn't want to examine my dad's body too closely for marks. Ew. "Er, well I don't really remember, do you, Dad?"

Dad looked at me and shook his head.

"What?" I said.

"You just called your son *Dad*, Mr. Stevenson," the doctor said quietly.

"My son?" I mentally kicked myself. Here I was complaining about Dad forgetting all the time that we'd swapped bodies, and I had gone and forgotten myself! *Still,* I thought to myself *if anyone should know, it would be Doctor Edwards.*

I looked at Dad. He seemed to understand what I was thinking. He shook his head slowly, obviously not wanting me to reveal what had happened. But then what was the point in coming to the doctor?

"Are you OK, Mr. Stevenson?" Doctor Edwards asked, a concerned look on his face. I glanced at Dad one more time. I clenched my fists and spoke.

"I'm not Mr. Stevenson!" I said, much louder than I had expected. Nothing happened. No explosions, no police cars, nothing. Maybe it wasn't so bad to tell him after all. He glanced at his computer again.

"My computer says you are unless you gave a false name? Because that's against the…"

"No, no, that's not what I mean," I began.

"It doesn't matter. He's crazy," Dad said. "We are here about being struck by lightning."

"Yes," I said. "*Exactly.* And when we were struck by lightning…."

"It hurt," Dad interrupted again, trying to stop me.

"We," I started.

"No, we didn't," Dad said.

"Swapped."

"Didn't happen," Dad interrupted again.

I sat and folded my arms. "You're being a pain, you know that?" I said to Dad.

"Welcome to *my life!*" Dad shouted back.

The doctor blinked as we stared daggers at each other. Slowly, he said, "Is there something you would like to share, Mr. Stevenson?"

"Yes," I said, sitting up in my chair. "There is."

Dad shook his head, "This isn't going to end well."

I didn't bother listening to my dad anymore. Here we were in front of a *trained professional*, someone who would know how to help us, and Dad *didn't* want to say anything because he might look a bit silly? No, I wasn't having it. I shifted myself to a comfortable position in my chair, looked the Doctor straight in the eyes and said, "I am not David Stevenson. I am his son, Jack Stevenson. David Stevenson is over there," I pointed at Dad. "We have *swapped bodies*. Can you help us? We don't know what to do."

Doctor Edwards suddenly looked incredibly interested in his computer screen again. He opened and closed his mouth a few times, scratched his head, rubbed his eyes and then turned back to us. "You've... swapped bodies..." he said.

"Yes," I nodded. "When the lightning struck us, we woke up in different bodies."

"You've..." he pointed at each of us in turn.

"This is going about as well as expected," Dad mumbled.

Doctor Edwards typed something into his computer. "Interesting," he mumbled to himself. "So you're, Jack?"

"Yes!" I said. We were finally getting somewhere!

"And you're...David?"

My dad shrugged. It didn't matter, the doc got the idea.

"Yes," I said. "Is there anything we can do? Like a pill? Or a cream? I mean, I don't *really* like taking pills, but if it means I can get out of this mess, I'm fine with it! Or is it an injection? Dad gets a little woozy around needles, so we might have to let him lie down first." My mouth was on overdrive at the possibility of finally getting this solved.

The doctor typed something into his computer and pressed print. Dad and I watched a small piece of paper come out of the device next to us. "What's this?" I asked.

"That," the doctor paused, "is the phone number of a Doctor James Turner. He's a specialist in...er... *these* sorts of cases. If you've really been struck by lightning."

"Oh really?" I said, grabbing the piece of paper. "So people have body swapped before?"

The doctor glanced at Dad. "Sort of."

I looked at Dad and then the doctor. They weren't telling me something. "What's up?"

"It's a psychiatrist, Jack. He thinks we are crazy." Dad stood up, putting on his coat. "This was a waste of time."

"But... but..." I frowned. "You said you were going to help us." I looked down at the piece of paper in my hand, betrayed.

"No, no, you aren't *crazy*," Doctor Edwards assured us. "You could be suffering from some kind of shock. I just think a specialist who knows how to deal with these issues…."

"Issues? We don't have issues! We just need help!" I felt myself begin to get angry. I threw the piece of paper on the floor. "Thanks for *nothing!*" I was furious as I stormed out of the room, the door crashing loudly against the wall as I flung it open. I didn't even turn when I heard the doctor calling after me. I just wanted to be out of there. Away from the liars.

I marched past the nurse, who asked me to stop as well, and kept going until I was sitting in the front seat of the car again, listening to the sound of my own breathing. What were we going to do? How were we going to solve this? I looked out the windscreen of the car, up at the sky. Night had fallen and I could see the stars against the inky black above me. I felt the fist clenching rage inside me subside and I let out a breath. There was only one thing we could do now. Go back home.

Skate Park Disaster

Once I had gotten home and calmed down, the doctor's office called us back. I now had an appointment with Dr. Turner in a couple of weeks' time at his office. I got to tell them I was *really excited* and then slammed the phone down without saying goodbye. It might not have been an *adult* thing to do, but it felt great. Even Dad didn't complain.

Luckily, the next day was Saturday, so we didn't have to worry about work or school. I lay in bed for a long time thinking about the future. What if this was *permanent*? What if I *was* crazy? I twisted and turned until I couldn't stay there any longer. I looked at the clock beside my bed. It was 8:30 am. *Great,* I thought to myself. *I can't even enjoy a lie-in in this body.*

Slumping out of bed, I wandered downstairs to find Dad already stood in the kitchen, cradling a cup of coffee in his hands. He looked up at me and then back down at his coffee before taking a sip. "Bleugh!" he spat it back out. "Ugh, something must have happened to the coffee, because this tastes *awful.*" He tipped the rest of it down the sink.

"Just one more thing to go wrong in our lives," I said, wandering into the living room and slumping down on the couch. I didn't know what to do, so I decided to do what I did best: video games.

The TV glowed in front of me as it powered up. I glanced up again at Dad who yawned at me from the doorway. "I'm going to make bacon and eggs. Want some?"

"Uh huh." I lay down on the couch with my feet dangling over the edge of the arm rest, my favorite gaming position.

A few hours and one plate of bacon and eggs later, the front door opened and a cold wind blew into the room. I frowned, peering over the top of the couch to see Tom stood in the doorway, looking confusedly between the lounge and the kitchen.

Dad was still doing the washing up.

"Jack, are you doing the washing up?" Tom asked, wandering into the kitchen. I shook my head into gear, slapping myself on the face to wake up. I leaped over the couch, landing with all the gracefulness of an elephant on the other side.

"Oof!" I saw stars for a second, before leaping again to my feet and following Tom into the kitchen.

"Er…yes," Dad said, looking at his foamy hands. "I've got to do my chores and stuff."

"Ah," Tom said. "That sucks."

"And I was just *testing out* Jack's games console because we thought it was broken," I added loudly before Tom thought anything was off.

Tom nodded with an uncomfortable smile, "That's great."

He turned back to Dad. "Did you forget that we were going to the Skate Park today Jack? Everyone's down there already and we wondered where you were."

The *Skate Park!* All the plans I had made (and then completely forgotten about) came flooding back like the world's worst headache.

"Yes! He remembered!" I said, jumping next to Dad and ruffling his hair in what I assumed was a Dad-like way. "I'm just being a normal, boring, very strict Dad and making him do his chores before he leaves. Aren't I the *worst?*" I grinned. Tom looked visibly worried.

Dad moved out from under my hand, trying to re-adjust his hair.

"I mean, you're just doing what any *loving* father would *do, Dad,*" he said back to me through gritted teeth.

"Nope," I said back to him. "I'm the worst! So, so awful."

"Yeah," Tom frowned. "Are you both OK?"

"One hundred percent!" I shouted. "In fact, I'm doing *so* well, I'll even take you to the Skate Park. Just let me get dressed!

"No, really, Mr. Stevenson, it's OK," Tom began to protest, but I had already left the room and was scampering upstairs. Sure, the Skate Park was within walking distance of our house, but I wasn't going to let Dad go off on his own with my friends. That would absolutely end in disaster!

What I didn't realize is that getting dressed would be a problem in itself. I looked in Dad's wardrobe at the different suits, shirts and *adult* clothes, all folded neatly or hanging from a hanger. I didn't know how he managed to keep it all in order, but it didn't work for me. I began to take things out and throw them onto the floor like a *normal* person would.

"No," I said, removing a blue shirt. "Nope," I threw some black pants over my shoulder. I looked at a Hawaiian shirt that Dad loved. "Nooooooo!" *That* deserved to be burned and nothing more. Finally, deep at the back of his wardrobe, underneath spider webs and a thick smell of dust, I found an old t-shirt and a worn pair of jeans. I *knew* I would find some eventually.

With a sigh of relief, I chucked them on and headed back downstairs where Tom and Dad waited uncomfortably by the door. "Let's rock and roll!" I said. In my new deeper voice, it sounded *awful*. I made a mental note never to say it again. Dad and Tom walked silently behind me.

The Skate Park was just around the corner from our house. It was a small relief because the drive there was *uncomfortable* and silent. Tom stared out the window and Dad was desperately clinging onto the door handle until his knuckles went white. I couldn't even brag to Tom about how *awesome* my driving skills were now (they were *super* awesome).

As I pulled into the parking lot next to the Skate Park, Tom couldn't get out of the car fast enough. I came to a stop and he leaped out, closing the door behind him. I decided to use this time to talk to Dad.

"Dad," I began.

"Listen, I know a few skating tricks from my youth, so this won't be terrible," he interrupted me. "Might even go well."

I snorted out a laugh. Yeah right.

"Just keep it short," I hissed back. "Make up an excuse and we'll go back home, as long as…oh, no." My eyes caught a flash of perfect blond hair floating towards us.

Dad turned to see what I was looking at. At the edge of the park, roller skating through the entrance was the one person I didn't want Dad to bump into. It was *Holly*. She did that cute little smile she is so good at and waved at Dad. He waved back uncomfortably.

"So is Holly your *girlfriend?*" Dad asked.

The question came out of nowhere. I started mumbling and stuttering. "W-w-what?" I said, feeling the heat rise to my face. "I mean, girlfriend is a strong word, we talk a lot and stuff, I mean if you want you *could* say that."

Dad nodded, "Uh huh. Girlfriend then. I'll try not to embarrass you." He then did the kind of smile that said: *I am absolutely going to embarrass you, but without meaning to.* That was, after all, Dad's specialty.

Too late, I thought as Dad got out of the car. I knew that I couldn't go anywhere while Holly was here. I sat in the car and watched Dad awkwardly greet her with a wave even though she was expecting a hug. It was painful. Tom and Holly offered me a polite wave too and I waved back. They then turned and headed into the Skate Park.

I looked down at the car keys in my hands. At this point, Dad would drive away and then come back in an hour or so. That's what I needed to do so they wouldn't suspect anything was up. Just start the engine and drive away. Easy.

I glanced at my friends again. Start the engine…Tom made a joke and Holly laughed. …and drive away…Dad just scratched his head uncomfortably. He didn't get it and was probably confused. *Ugh,* I thought to myself. *He's barely been here two minutes and he's already messing it up!*

I shoved the keys into my jean's pocket. I had no choice. I was going to follow them in.

No Adults Allowed

I had been coming to this Skate Park since I was six. I had got a skateboard for my birthday (a tiny one made of plastic) and really wanted to test it out. Since then, this place had become like a second home to me.

I knew the steps where I had fallen down, cut my knee, and everyone had thought I was really brave because I didn't cry. I knew the corner where Tom first attempted to climb the 'unclimbable' wall.

He didn't succeed, but he still holds the record for getting up the highest. I knew the small hut in the corner which people say is haunted by the skaters who have died here and no one will go close to when it gets dark.

As I entered through the front gate this time, it felt *different*. I felt like Neil Armstrong stepping onto the moon for the first time. To begin with, everything was smaller. Once epic-looking half pipes and grinding rails now looked alright, if a little sad. The high, concrete walls that surrounded the park now looked like I could easily climb them. There was no sense of awesomeness or comfort. It felt unnatural like someone had taken my favorite place, shrunk it down and covered it in *boring* paint.

I stood out like a sore thumb. Teenagers roamed in packs around here. Tall, thin, and dressed in dark clothing with piercings that looked more uncomfortable than practical. Some of them had even started *shaving* and liked to flaunt their new chin hairs. They stood in little groups in different parts of the Skate Park, usually corners where they could huddle together and laugh at everyone else. But now they weren't laughing. They were *watching* me as I went past. I felt like a gazelle on one of those nature programs my Dad loves so much. They were the lions.

As if to prove my point even more, spray painted on a nearby wall, surrounded by a clump of teens were the words:

DEFF TOO ADULTS!

and

NO ADULTS ALOUD

I think what they meant was 'Death to Adults' and 'No adults allowed,' but I wasn't going to go up and ask them. Normally, I would have looked at the spray paint and smiled, but today I was an *adult*. I was trespassing on their land. It wasn't my land anymore. I started walking a bit faster. Better to get this over with quickly, I decided.

I found my friends and Dad right at the back of the park (as far away from me as they could possibly get, obviously). But I couldn't have prepared myself for what I saw.

Dad wasn't a *complete* loser when he was younger. Just like me, he really enjoyed skating. It turned out, even though it had been years since he had been on a board, he still had some skills! Crowds of kids gathered around the half pipe as he dropped into it. He swung down and then flew up the other side, using the momentum to launch into the air and... He flipped, grabbed the edge of his board and twisted in the air, a move I had never seen before!

"*OOOOOOOOOOOHHHHhhhhh,*" said the crowd watching him.

He came up the other side and did another trick, this time saluting the crowd *while in the air.*

"*AAAAAAAAAAaaaahhhh!*" the crowd said again, bursting out into applause. I even found myself pausing to watch what was going on. I didn't want to admit, it but my Dad was actually being pretty… cool. I would never tell him I thought that, of course.

He kept going for a few more minutes and then he finally stopped, stamping on the edge of the skate board, making it flip into his hand. The crowd let out one final cheer and Dad waved at them before turning to my friends with a wild grin on his face. My face.

Something twisted inside of me when I saw that Dad was actually having *fun* with my friends. I'd expected him to have the worst day of his life, just like me. Holly ran down into the half pipe to my Dad and wrapped her arms around him.

"That was awesome!" I heard her shout and my Dad, after recovering from the shock of the hug, grinned even wider and hugged her back. The thing inside me twisted again. A small voice in my head whispered: She never hugged *you* like that.

That's when I realized I was jealous of my *Dad*! It was crazy. I tried to shake it off. *In a few days, everything will be back to normal,* I told myself. *I will be hanging out here with my friends like usual. Everything will be fine. FINE.*

But as I watched Holly continue to hug him, I knew I was lying to myself. How did I know that anything would be normal again? What if I was stuck like this *forever?*

The thing inside me popped an evil thought into my mind. If Dad was acting like me, I decided I was going to act like *Dad*.

"Jack!" I shouted, making my way towards the half pipe.

Dad and Holly both turned to look at me. Holly stepped away from Dad, her cheeks going red. I saw her whisper to him: "What is your Dad doing here, Jack?" I didn't give him a chance to respond.

When I reached him, I put a hand on his shoulder and said: "I'm proud of you, son. That skating was really *rad*."

It worked like a charm. An *uncool* bomb was set off at his feet and spread around the Skate Park. Any cool points he had just achieved were instantly destroyed by a parent getting involved. Parents are the opposite of anything cool. The reaction was most visible in Tom's face as he stood at the edge of the half pipe. He flinched like he had just bitten into a lemon. Holly stepped further away, trying to escape from the damage I had caused.

Dad, however, seemed oblivious to the whole thing. He looked up at me with a big, wide grin, like he had just received the best compliment of his life! What was *wrong* with him? He was such a *weirdo*.

"Thanks," he said. "That's really kind."

No, I thought. *Not a weirdo. An uncool adult.*

Then, to make things worse for himself, he hugged *me!* I couldn't believe it! It couldn't have worked out better!

And yet for some reason, I felt…bad. Not because I had just ruined my own reputation (that little fact wouldn't occur to me until much later). No, it was the fact that Dad was happy, I was proud of him. It was actually something that he wanted, not something he thought was uncool.

"Er," I said, stepping back. "We've got to go, something has come up."

Dad looked at Holly and Tom, who were whispering to each other. "I'm sorry guys, I've gotta go!"

"Ok," Holly said. "See you later."

"That you will," Dad replied, and then he *winked* at her. Holly bit back a laugh. I cringed inside. Dad was trying to *help* again. I hate it when he does that.

The car journey home was quiet. I kept running the events at the Skate Park through my head. I still felt like I had done something *wrong*. It was so weird.

"You alright?" Dad broke the silence as we pulled into our drive.

I shrugged. "Alright as I can be."

"Well, why did we leave early? I thought I was doing a pretty decent job."

Yeah, I thought to myself sadly, *of stealing my friends.* But I said something else: "I realized there was something else we need to prepare for. Probably your biggest test yet."

Dad looked at me like a lost puppy. "What do I have to do now?" he whined. "Being a kid wasn't *this* confusing when I was your age."

"Well, tomorrow," I said solemnly, "is band practice."

Band Practice

Dad stood near the drum kit in our garage holding a drum stick in each hand. He looked at the different-sized drums and cymbals in front of him.

"What do you think?" I asked.

"How hard can it be?" He grinned and raised the sticks into the air like some kind of nerdy rock star. "Let's rock!" Then he started to play.

When I played the drums, I was a well-oiled machine. I could feel the beat of the music running through me and the drums were my heartbeat. In fact, that's why I formed my band. Me on drums, Holly with the singing voice of an angel, and Tom who could strum a few chords on his guitar. Together we sounded awesome.

I could tell that this next band practice wasn't going to be the same. Dad on the drums was like a confused octopus who couldn't tell left from right.

"No!" I said, forcing him to stop. I pointed at the round snare drum directly in front of him. "You hit that one twice and *that* one," I pointed at large bass drum below him, "four times. Not the other way around."

Dad shrugged. "Does it *really* matter?"

I wanted to pull out my hair. He was so *frustrating*. "Of course it matters!"

Dad sighed. "Alright, let's have a go again."

It continued like this for the rest of the day. It took me a few hours to get a basic rock beat into his mind before he gave up because he was "tired". He wandered off back into the house, despite my encouraging him to continue. "Do you *want* me to look stupid?" I shouted after him. He ignored me.

It was like he was actively trying to fail. At this rate, he would *never* convince my friends that we weren't body swapped.

The next morning, I was pacing around the house, nervously. Dad calmly sat in front of the TV watching the news.

"This is a terrible idea," I said. "We should call them and...."

The doorbell rang. I almost jumped out of my skin.

Dad rolled his eyes and went to open the door, but I grabbed his shoulder stopping him. "What if we pretend we're not here?"

Dad leaned close to me. "They can see us through the window, Jack."

I looked up. On the other side of the door, Holly and Tom stood chatting to each other. I let go of Dad and forced a fake smile onto my face.

"Oh," I whispered. I opened the door, silently reminding myself that we needed to appear *normal*. Like nothing was different. Sunday was band practice. It always had been.

"Hello, Jack's friends," I said. *That sounded natural, right?* I thought to myself. "Welcome again to this house that you have been to before." The nerves were affecting my brain. It was like I was in the kindergarten nativity all over again. I was a star then and forgot my one line: "The child is born!" and instead said: "I'm tired and bored." My acting career went down the drain before I knew it.

"Oh," Holly said uncomfortably. "Hello, Mr. Stevenson, is Jack in?"

I sighed quietly. "Yeah, he's here. Are you planning on doing band practice?"

"Yes, Mr. Stevenson. I hope that's OK," Tom said. Every time he called me 'Mr. Stevenson,' it was like being poked with a pin. It felt wrong on so many levels. Dad joined me by the door.

"Head into the garage guys, I'll see you there," Dad said. Holly and Tom set off. He turned to me. "Don't worry, it'll all be fine. I'll pretend to hurt my hand or something."

I nodded. Everything was fine. We had a **plan**.

Five minutes later, I could tell everything *wasn't* fine. I was listening to my band through the door, and it sounded like Dad had somehow gotten *even worse* even though I had told him what to do. At the end of the first song ("Why must you steal my video games?" by the Spiky Monkeys, a classic) Tom was already annoyed by Dad.

"What was *that*?" Tom said. "Has your brain stopped working?"

"I just need to…er…warm up," Dad said, pathetically. "My hands are cramping."

"Warm up?" Holly asked. "You don't usually need to."

That was it. It was time for damage control. I stepped into the room with my best Dad grin, making everyone jump. "How's it going, guys? Sounds like you're *rockin out hard!*" I tried not to look too disgusted at what I had just said, maintaining the grin on my face.

"Are you OK, Mr. Stevenson?" Holly said. "You look a bit... strange." She glanced at Dad. I knew that look. It meant *PLEASE GET YOUR DAD OUT OF HERE AS SOON AS POSSIBLE.* Unfortunately, I wasn't planning on moving. Instead, I found the nearest clear space and sat down on it.

"Why don't you play me a song?" I asked. "I've always been interested to hear you guys play."

"Really?" Dad asked. "You've never come in before. You've given us. Our. Space." As he said the last few words, Dad pointed his head towards the door. He wanted me to leave. I didn't move.

"I guess I was a bad parent up until now because I'm super interested!" I grinned. "Go on, I won't mind."

"We're still practicing," Holly said quietly. I felt a little bad at putting her on the spot, especially as she didn't really like performing, but there was *no way* I was leaving my Dad in here alone with them.

"That's OK, I understand," I said, still not moving. Tom glanced at Dad, who shrugged.

"Let's…*sigh*…rock then," Dad said with a roll of the eyes. "1,2,3,4."

He didn't even count them in right. Holly and Tom started together, but Dad came in too fast. I had told him, again and again, to start after 4, but he always began playing too soon.

"My games are all I need," Holly sang in her perfect voice.

Twang twangalang, Tom rocked out on guitar.

Thump CRASH bang. Dad stumbled across the drum kit.

"But you took them away…" Holly cringed as she tried to keep going.

Twangle twang twang. Tom looked like the sound actually hurt him.

Thummmmmmmmmm**p.** Dad was grinning and having a good time. Of *course* he was.

"Now they are gone, I don't know what to say,"Holly began the rise towards the chorus when….

"LOOK OUT!" Dad shouted. One of his drumsticks flew right out of his hand as he hit the drum too hard. Time seemed to slow and everyone could only look on in horror as it flew through the air and- CLONK.

It smacked Holly right between the eyes!

She stumbled away from the microphone, stunned for a moment before finally raising her hand to her forehead. "Ow!" she said. "What's *wrong* with you today, Jack?"

My dad got up, eyes wide with embarrassment. "I'm sorry!" he said over and over. "I'm so, so sorry!"

I stood up as well, walking over to her. "Are you OK Holly? Do you need anything? A plaster? A hug?" I held my arms out. Holly looked at me like I was Frankenstein's Monster.

"I think I just want to go home," she said, tears forming in her eyes and she ran out of the room.

"Holly, wait!" I shouted after her.

Tom was quick to follow. "I'll make sure she gets home OK, Mr. Stevenson," he said too quickly. "Jack, you've got to get your head in the game!" he added quietly, before leaving the garage and going back into the house.

"Jack," Dad began. "I'm sorry I thought I...."

"Just save it," I snapped. I didn't want to hear his excuses. Once again, he had ruined everything. I stormed out of the room after my friends, leaving Dad sitting behind the drum kit, staring at the remaining drumstick in his hand.

I tried to catch up with Holly, to tell her that I was really sorry and that Dad had, I didn't know. I was running out of excuses. Luckily (I suppose), Holly and Tom were long gone by the time I reached the front door. The house was empty and quiet. I sighed and went upstairs. I'd had enough of today. I'd had enough of everything.

Mr. Stevenson, teacher, expert

Mondays. No one likes Mondays and for good reasons. The weekend is over and you have to start a *boring* week all over again. Of course, I didn't expect my week to start quite like this.

I sat behind Dad's desk at school and stared at his empty classroom, listening to the sounds of students yelling and playing outside. His classroom suddenly looked a lot bigger and scarier than I was used to. I looked towards the door. His class would be coming in shortly. The *other* 7th-grade class. The door looked a million miles away. I had no chance to escape.

"It'll be fine," Dad said, placing a stack of papers on the desk next to me. "We can't afford to miss any more days."

"I definitely can," I said, trying to ignore my shaking hands. Suddenly, the thought of being a teacher didn't seem so hilarious or fun.

"Just follow the **plan** and everything will be fine," Dad said, tapping the paper on the desk in front of me.

That's right. We had a **plan**. Considering how well the last **plan** went, I didn't have high hopes for this one either. At least Dad couldn't walk in and mess it up. I looked down at my scribbled handwriting again, to double check I knew what was happening:

*Morning – **Math** (ugh) - Get students to do the <u>worksheet</u> (the one Dad printed out). I just need to sit at the front and watch them work.*

Break – You are on duty! Go outside and stand around. Look like a teacher who knows what he is doing. (Find students who are having too much fun and tell them to stop. <u>Teachers do not like fun!</u>)

*Before Lunch – **Geography** – Students have a 'map project' to finish. Get them to do it. (They should know what 'map project' means)*

Lunch – Eat lunch. Chicken sandwich and a candy bar for energy.

*After lunch – **History** – Get them to write an essay on the Fall of the Roman Empire! (No talking, no laughing, no enjoying. No happiness. School and happiness do not mix)*

My phone buzzed in my pocket and I looked at the message. "Tom is looking for me...you...you as me, at the front of the school."

Dad nodded, "Don't worry, I'll stay quiet all day, say I have a sore throat."

I nodded. It was for the best. If Dad couldn't speak, he couldn't say anything *stupid.*

"I won't forget to pick up your homework either," Dad grinned, punching me playfully in the arm.

Yay. Homework! Uggh!

As he left the room, I let out a breath. I could do this. Teaching would be *easy.*

Teaching, it turned out, wasn't that easy. After the students came in and settled in for the morning, they wouldn't sit down and just do the worksheet! Nooooo! They kept coming up to me and asking me questions.

First, it was Sally Bride: "Mr. Stevenson, what's thirty-five divided by seven?"

I didn't know. I had to use a calculator and then Sally asked why *she* couldn't use a calculator. "Because you're not old enough!" I said, sending her back to her chair.

Ken Matthews then came up to me *barely a second later* saying, "Mr. Stevenson, I accidentally dropped my worksheet out of the window, can I have another one?" In the course of the lesson, I had to get him ten new sheets, until I realized it would just be easier to close the window he sat next to.

Every five minutes there was also: "Mr. Stevenson, why do I have to stand and face the corner? What have I done wrong?"

Just stand and face the corner, Tommy Wilkins!" I said for the hundredth time, secretly grinning. "I'm your *teacher*. You have to do *as I say.*" I sat back in the chair behind the desk and let out a sigh. Who knew teaching was so *tiring*?

When the bell finally rang for break, I let out a long sigh of relief. So did the class. I waved them off to break without saying a word and slumped my head down onto the desk, scattering hastily collected worksheets everywhere. Teaching was *lame.* I opened one eye and looked back into the classroom.

"Oh," I said. "You can go to break too, Tommy."

The boy turned back from the corner, let out a whoop of joy and ran out of the room. I'd always thought being in control would be fun, but it was like trying to balance plates on sticks but the plates and sticks keep asking you *why* you are balancing them and *how long* you plan to balance them and a thousand other questions. I glanced down at the **plan** again and groaned.

I was on yard duty. Would this day *never end?* I got up, picking up my coat, and slowly trudged outside after the class.

Break time

The sky was gray and the wind was blowing. Unlike all the students who got to run around and keep warm, I had to stand still and hug myself, hoping my Dad's thin coat would protect me from hypothermia. I stared longingly at a colorful poster which hung on a nearby wall and read it.

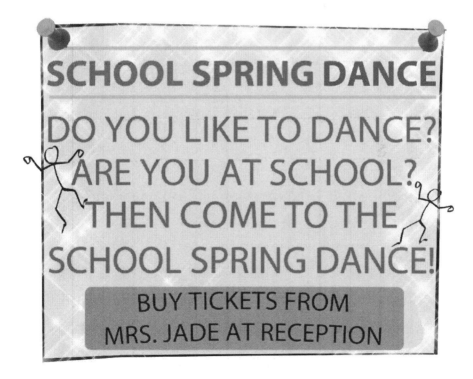

The poster was covered in glitter, sparkles, and had pictures of stick men dancing on it. The dance committee, run by some tenth graders and the drama teacher, Miss White, had really gone all out this year. Glitter pens don't grow on trees after all.

The dance…it was only a few weeks away. It was when the cool kids got to be their coolest. Naturally, I would have been one of the stars of the dance. I looked down at the body I was in. I looked at the tight, uncomfortable shirt and tie that Dad had made me wear and the black shoes that pinched my feet. How did *anyone* wear stuff like this?

"Mr. Stevenson," Samantha, a small girl from eighth grade, ran up to me.

Go away!" I snapped.

She stared up at me with big brown eyes that slowly filled with tears and then she ran away. *Oops.*

I considered going after her and making sure she was alright when I caught sight of Holly and Tom hanging out on a bench nearby. I started to head towards them and then remembered who I was, so I hung back. They didn't look happy. I frowned. Where was Dad? Holly looked up across the yard and I followed her gaze.

"Oh, no!" I said out loud.

If there was one person I *didn't* want my Dad hanging out with in the entire school, it was *Jasmine Walder*. So guess who he was currently standing next to on the far side of the yard and actually *talking* to? You got it. *Jasmine Walder*. She was part of the nerdy gang who thought they were better than everyone else because they had such *good grades*.

Why did I want to avoid her specifically? Well, that's another story.

This had taken place a few years earlier when Matthew Lane brought in a GAMEKID 3D™. Nowadays, the GAMEKID 3D™ is an old console. Since then, they have released the GAMEKID MINI 3D™, the GAMEKID- PRO 3D™ and even more recently the GAMEKID 3D VIRTUAL PLUS™ (which is super awesome, I've been trying to get my dad to buy me one for weeks). But when this happened, the GAMEKID 3D™ had only just come out and I *really* wanted a go. Matthew even had the ADVENTURES OF KRON, which was (and still is) the *best game ever made ever!*

I begged Matthew to let me have a go. I said I would do *anything*. I would buy him candy, I would give him my toys, *anything*.

Matthew was one of those kids who liked to make mischief, so he said that he would let me go if I completed his dare. Naturally, I said yes!

He said, "I DARE YOU TO KISS JASMINE WALDER!"

I was reluctant at first, but Tom told me if I didn't do the dare, not only would I not be able to play the GAMEKID 3D™, but I would also be labeled as Jack, King of the Wimps, for all of eternity.

So I did it. I walked over to Jasmine on that same break with all my friends watching, smiled sweetly at her and said: "Hey Jasmine, you're looking great and stuff,"

(I was a smooth talker, even then) and when Jasmine blushed and said thank you, I closed my eyes, held my breath, puckered up and *kissed her on the cheek.*

(If you're wondering, the GAMEKID 3D™ was absolutely worth it. But that's not the point.)

I would take it back if I could because since then Jasmine Walder has been *obsessed* with me. She always tries to talk to me, she tries to be my partner in *everything,* and I've been told that her books are covered in doodles saying JACK & JASMINE 4EVA in little pink hearts.

It sends a shiver down my spine just thinking about it.

As I considered how to deal with the situation (could I just lock Jasmine in a cupboard? Are teachers allowed to do that?), I sidestepped closer to Holly and Tom to eavesdrop on their conversation. I was careful to stare in the other direction so they wouldn't know I was listening.

"I don't *get* it," Tom said. "Why is he acting like that?"

"I don't know," Holly said. "He acted as if I didn't exist today."

"But he's your boyfriend!"

"Yeah, I mean, I *thought* he was..."

"Has he asked you to the dance yet?"

"No," Holly said quietly.

My heart sank in my chest. Holly was having second thoughts about us and it was *all because of Dad.* I knew we should have stayed home again today, but no, Dad really wanted to go in. I bit my tongue, trying to stop myself from screaming in frustration.

"Maybe he's ill?" Tom tried to talk Holly back from where she was going.

"Or maybe he just sucks. I'm going back inside." As Holly ran past me, I could see tears in her eyes.

It was too much. I had to take action and I had to do it now. I set off towards Dad.

Jasmine's laugh echoed across the yard. It was a nasal, screechy laugh which made my ears sting the closer I got. Her brown pig-tails bobbed as she and Dad continued their conversation and she stared intensely at him. Could Dad not see what he was doing? Was he really this blind?

"Jack Stevenson!" I shouted in a voice that had been used so many times against me. It felt weird to command it myself. "Come over here, please." I felt *weird* using my voice like that, but it got Dad's attention. He walked over to me, frowning.

"What?" he asked.

"What? *What?*" I almost squeaked. "What are you *doing?* Why aren't you with Tom and Holly?"

Dad glanced over at Tom on the bench. "Jasmine sat down next to me in class and, well, I think she's a really nice girl. You could use more friends like her, Jack."

"I don't *need* 'more friends like her'," I hissed at him. "I already have friends. You know, Tom and Holly? Not Jasmine and her crew. This isn't how it works here."

Dad frowned, glancing back at Jasmine. She waved.

"I think that Jasmine and her "crew," as you put it, are wonderful students," Dad said stubbornly.

"But they're not cool and I am. I can't be *seen* with them or I'll be bullied."

"Maybe if you hang out with them more, they will get more "cool" and won't be bullied as much," Dad said, folding his arms.

He wasn't listening to me, again. It felt like a one-sided conversation. But this time, he didn't have all the power. *I did!*

"Jasmine," I said in my best teacher voice, side stepping Dad. "Mr. Thomas was looking for you inside."

Jasmine's eyes snapped up to me. She looked panicked, unprepared to be talked to by a teacher. "Yes, Mr. Stevenson!" she squeaked before dashing off to see what her precious Mr. Thomas wanted.

Dad sighed behind me. "That was very rude of you, Jack," he said, shaking his head. "We are going to talk about this later.

I looked him dead in the eye and scowled at him.

"No," I said, "we aren't." And with that, I turned and stormed off.

Lessons are Boring

I was still angry after lunch, and it was time to 'teach' history now. I looked down at Dad's **plan**. The students were meant to write an essay on the fall of the Roman Empire. I clenched my fists and, in a moment of anger, I crumpled the piece of paper into a little ball and threw it in the nearby waste bin. School was boring enough without *essays*.

It felt strangely freeing, throwing away the **plan**. I suddenly realized I could do *anything I wanted* now. There was nothing Dad could do, there was nothing *anyone* could do because, after all, I was the teacher. A small grin burst out on my face as the students began to drag themselves in from lunch. I could see on their faces the fear of a long, boring afternoon, but I had other plans.

I was living the life every kid at school had dreamed about during a hot sunny day of pop-quizzes and surprise tests. I was the *teacher*. I held the power. I was king.

Raising my feet, I put them up on the desk and leaned back on my hands. "Ahhh," I let out a long, comfortable sigh. I could already see a few of the students looking around, wondering what was wrong.

What had happened to their *normal, boring* Mr. Stevenson?

He was long gone.

I yawned loudly and checked my fingernails for dirt. "Everyone have fun at lunch?"

There was a bored murmur from the class saying yes.

"Want to keep having fun?"

The students said, "Yes!" but were unsure. I knew what was going through their heads. What did their teacher have planned? A pop quiz? Another exam?

I smiled at them. "Go on then. Do what you want."

The students stared back at me. They didn't know what to say. Not even smarty pants Tommy Wilkins, who usually had an answer for everything.

"I'm going to take a nap," I said. "Don't make *too* much of a mess." With that, I placed a history book over my eyes and leaned back into my chair.

Nobody moved in the classroom. They still thought it was too good to be true. I started making snoring noises. **ZZZZZZZZZZzzzzzz *snort* zzzZZZZZZZzzzzz.**

Still, nobody moved.

I took the book off my face. The students all stared at me like a herd of deer caught in front of headlights. I rolled my eyes. "Come on guys, don't just sit there. You can do *whatever you want*. I don't care. You won't get in trouble."

Realization slowly spread across the class that I wasn't joking. As if to test out the theory, Johnny Jacobs slowly stood up at the back of the class and then, via his chair, climbed on top of the desk, standing taller than everyone else in the room. Tommy gasped in horror.

I nodded. "Johnny's got the right idea. Good on you, Johnny."

Johnny grinned like it was Christmas. When Dad had been teaching, I don't think he ever praised Johnny like that. But I was in charge now!

Other students slowly began to catch on. There was a murmur of a conversation starting in one corner. Another student pulled out his phone and started playing games on it, and then *finally* everyone started to do what they wanted. Windows were opened and Ken started dumping worksheets out of them. Sally put on some music and began to dance, people laughed and joked.

Fat Gary in the corner (his name wasn't *actually* fat Gary, but everyone called him that - even his Mom) was surrounded by an increasing mountain of candy wrappers as if he was trying to eat twice his weight in them.

I sat back in my chair and watched it all. I was definitely the coolest teacher around.

Everything was going great.

It was around the point when the students formed a conga line and started knocking books off shelves and stationary onto the floor that it happened.

KNOCK, KNOCK, KNOCK.

I didn't hear it at first. I was too busy listening to a Spiky Monkey album on my phone. But the second time it was louder and more insistent.

KNOCK, KNOCK, KNOCK.

The room fell silent.

Everyone looked at me.

I pushed myself out of my chair and crossed the room, opening the door slightly and peering around to see who it was.

It was the last person I wanted to see.

The frowning, angry face of the principal, Mrs. Kent, stared back at me. "Mr. Stevenson! What is the meaning of all this racket?"

I paused, holding the door slightly closed so she couldn't see inside. "Er… history?" I said with a smile.

Mrs. Kent didn't seem impressed. "It sounds like you're trying to destroy the school!" she said, her eyebrows twitching. "What *are* you doing in there?"

She tried to enter the room, but I held the door closed. Her face turned red and she looked at me as if she was about to explode.

"Ee, just, give me a second," I smiled sweetly, closing the door in her face.

Panic flooded through my body. How was I going to explain all this to the principal? Could I pretend to pass out? Maybe climb out of the window? I searched Dad's desk for anything that could help me. There was nothing except Dad's stupid history books. How were they going to…

BING. A light bulb lit up in my mind.

"Annnnnnnd stop," I shouted at the class. They all looked at me, perplexed. "Well done guys, that was a good demonstration of the *barbarians* who destroyed the Roman Empire. Out of control. Disaster. Very, very good."

The students looked at each other and at the mess of the room they had made around them.

I clapped my hands together. "Now, let's pretend we're the Roman Empire. Tidy up! Last person with a tidy table gets detention!"

Panic fluttered throughout the room as the students started to swarm around, tidying up everything.

My heart was beating fast too because, at that same time, Mrs. Kent flung open the door and strode into the room.

"What's going on in here!" she shouted.

The class, now sitting at tidy tables, stared back at her.

"History, Mrs. Kent," Tommy Wilkins smiled sweetly.

I smiled at the principal. "Yes! Well done, Tommy."
Maybe having a nerd in the class wasn't *too* awful.

Mrs. Kent narrowed her eyes and looked around the
room for anything suspicious. She turned to me. "I see,"
she said quietly.

It was at this exact moment that Gary decided that
he had eaten too much candy while pretending to be a
barbarian, and threw up all over his desk in a large
eruption of vomit!

The girls near him jumped up, screaming. Other
students tried to take photos with their phones.

It was *gross*.

Mrs. Kent looked at me with a raised eyebrow.

"I don't suppose you want to clean that up?" I
asked.

"I believe *that* duty falls to the teacher," she said
with a sneer, raising her nose and walking out of the
room.

"Of course," I sighed.

The rest of the day was filled with...you got it,
worksheets. Gary was sent home and it took me hours of
wiping and cleaning to get rid of the lumps he had
sprayed everywhere. By the end of the day, I was more

tired than I had ever been and couldn't get the smell of vomit out of my nose.

When the final bell rang, I said a silent prayer and told the class to leave. Teaching, I decided, was awful.

I gathered up my things as quickly as possible and left the classroom, heading towards Dad's (or my) classroom. As I went through the hallway, I heard something which sounded a lot like shouting.

"Admit it!" It sounded like Mr. Thomas. I would recognize that goblin-like tone anywhere.

"I won't because it's not true!" The other voice surprised me. It was Dad!

In Trouble

By the time I reached the source of the shouting, I found Mr. Thomas pointing an accusing finger at Dad. His face was starting to turn red, clearly from all the yelling he had been doing. I had never seen him this angry before! What had Dad done?

Dad, however, was giving as good as he got. He was also red in the face and stood, arms folded, staring angrily at Mr. Thomas.

"You're lying and I know it!" Mr. Thomas shouted.

"I'm not!" Dad shouted back. "Why are you not *listening* to me?"

Mr. Thomas was going purple now. I was sure that he would explode if no one stepped in. I was quite happy to stand back and watch it happen, but sadly he saw me.

"Mr. Stevenson! Mr. Stevenson!" he said, plodding over to me and grabbing me quite tightly by the arm. "Your son is answering back to a teacher! He is *questioning my authority*!"

I tried not to laugh. "So?"

Mr. Thomas's eyes bulged. "Well…well, he cheated on the math exam! He got an A+!" Mr. Thomas wiggled a piece of paper in front of my eyes. "He had *never* got higher than a D, and that was on a *really* good day!"

Oh *no*! The Math exam? The exam that would let me play in the first match of the season? I realized I had to do some serious damage control here.

Dad folded his arms and looked at Mr. Thomas stubbornly. "If he can find *evidence* that I cheated, then I will gladly accept the punishment."

"Now, Jack," I quickly stepped in. "You don't *usually* get A+ on an exam, do you? You can see why Mr. Thomas might be a bit *confused*." I tried to give him a look that said: *YOU WEREN'T MEANT TO DO SO WELL. YOU WERE SUPPOSED TO JUST DO IT AGAIN AND GET A LOWER MARK.* I'll admit, it was a tough one to pull off. There was a lot of eyebrow wiggling.

Mr. Thomas spun back around to Dad. "I don't need evidence! I am your teacher, I *know* it is true. You will be in detention for the rest of the week so you can realize that we do not allow *cheaters* in my classroom."

I was about to speak up in Dad's defense, but then I had a thought. If Dad was in detention, then he couldn't mess anything else up with Holly or Jasmine. Dad looked at me pleadingly. It was a look I had given to Dad so many times during my life. One he had ignored. I knew exactly how Dad would have responded. And besides, I talked to him before the test about the grade I should get. Even though he wanted me to get top marks, I knew it wouldn't look right. He only had himself to blame!

I nodded politely and said to him: "I think this is for the best, son. You need to take responsibility for your actions."

Dad's mouth dropped open. I tried not to burst out laughing there and then. It was *priceless*. I nodded to Mr. Thomas, who seemed very pleased with the situation and disappeared back into his room. Dad fought for words but none would come out. Now he would *definitely* understand what it was like to be me.

"Come on," I said cheerfully. "You've got to get to football practice!"

Dad didn't say anything until much later when we stood outside the changing rooms. He turned to me, eyes filled with fury, and demanded to know, "Why didn't you stand up to Mr. Thomas?"

I blinked at him. Wasn't it obvious? "You wouldn't have if it was me."

"But you *knew* I wasn't cheating."

"Isn't knowing all the answers already kind of cheating?"

Dad opened his mouth and closed it again. I had got him with that one. "I see," he said quietly and went inside the changing room. I knew what he was feeling. Betrayed, hurt, completely alone. I knew because I had felt like that so many times before. It was like the adults just *didn't understand me.*

Except I did understand. Did that make me worse? I shook my head and decided not to think about it as I headed towards the field.

Date Night

Football practice was *awful*. Dad had no skill whatsoever. He kept dropping the ball, he ran in the wrong direction, and that field goal technique I had perfected last week? Dad just dropped the ball and managed to kick *himself* instead. All I could do was watch and cringe and try not to scream. To make things worse, Holly and Jasmine were both watching! I thought maybe I could get close to Holly, make up some kind of excuse as to why 'Jack' had been acting so weird. I ran through a few in my mind. Jack wasn't getting enough sleep? Jack was actually a superhero by night? Jack was abducted by aliens?

It didn't matter, by the time I was close to her, a noise on the field made me turn. Dad had fallen over again. I rolled my eyes. He deserved to....

That was when I saw it. Jasmine was *running onto the field*. She ran over to my dad and hugged him, trying to help him up. Dad smiled and nodded as she talked to him, probably telling him how great he was. It was *terrible*!

Then I remembered that Holly was watching as well! I turned, quickly, to say something, anything, to make things right, but it was too late. She was gone.

After the game, I waited for Dad to get changed. When he finally emerged from the changing room I shook my head.

"That was…" I couldn't even find the word I was looking for. Dad didn't say anything, he just looked up at me and then moved on.

As we got in the car, there was a *tap tap tap*, on the window. Outside stood a woman with brown hair tied neatly into a ponytail at the side of her head. She wore a flowery dress. It was Sarah, Tom's mom. I lowered the window.

"Hi, Sarah!" I said. "What's up?"

"I see you're feeling better, David. That's good to see! How would you like come around to my place tonight? Make up for missing that date last week?"

"Er…well…I mean…." I wasn't sure how to say *NO* in a polite way. Unfortunately, Sarah took my hesitation to mean, *Oh yes, absolutely!*

"Brilliant! Just drive on over to our house and we'll see you there!" She smiled and walked away from the car.

I glanced back at Dad who was sitting, wide-eyed, watching her go.

"I guess we're going to Tom's!" I said cheerfully. Dad sank down in his chair.

"This is going to be terrible," he whispered.

"A bit like you today then," I said back, starting the engine. Dad didn't reply.

I was getting the hang of driving now. It only took us twenty minutes to get to Tom's house because I managed to drive at a sustained 20 miles per hour. Dad had taken to covering his eyes so he couldn't see what was going on, which helped.

Tom's house was large and old. It looked a bit like one of those haunted houses you see in films, with pointed roofs and three floors. It even had a basement (where Tom refused to go because he was *sure* there was something down there). We rang the doorbell and a series of loud, ominous DING DONGs echoed around the house. I glanced at Dad, who shrugged.

"Let's just keep this quick and simple," Dad whispered. "No stress, nice and…."

The door opened. Sarah and Tom stood on the other side. "Hello," Sarah smiled. "Took you a while to get here!"

"Er... car issues," I said. "What's for dinner?" I suddenly realized that I was *starving*. The day had really taken its toll on my stomach! It growled quietly. I hoped she had prepared something big.

"I don't know!" Sarah said. "I bought all the items you told me to buy. What are you planning to make?"

My stomach growled again, in anger. Dad had a weird habit. He *enjoyed* cooking. He is such a weirdo. But that meant I now had to cook dinner at Sarah's house. She pointed towards the kitchen and I felt myself go pale. "Right," I said quietly. "I'll go and cook...."

"I'll go with you!" Dad said quickly.

I frowned and then slowly nodded. "Yes, son. Come and learn from your old dad!"

"You're not *that* old, Dad!" he said with a big, forced laugh.

"I'm *pretty old,* son. I might even have to buy a walking stick soon!"

Dad shot me a look telling me to be quiet. I grinned back at him.

Sarah clapped her hands. "Oh, fantastic! Both of the Stevenson chefs working together!"

Dad followed me into the kitchen. It was way bigger than ours, and cleaner too. I stared at the ingredients neatly left on the side.

"Shall I open some wine?" Sarah asked, waving a bottle at me.

"Well," I began.

"No!" Dad shouted, "No wine!"

Sarah jumped in shock. I laughed. "Don't listen to him, he's just excited. I would *love* a glass of wine." After all, it looked like grape juice. It probably tasted the same too.

"I'll go get some glasses," Sarah jogged out of the room.

"What are you *doing?*" Dad snapped. "Are you trying to ruin everything?"

"You mean like you have been doing with my life so far?" I snapped back. "It's like everything I *tell* you to do, you go and do the complete opposite."

"Well, maybe my way is *better!*" Dad argued.

"Well, maybe *my* way of living *your* life is better!" I said as Sarah came back into the room.

"Is everything OK?" she asked.

"Perfecto!" I said with a grin. "I'm just giving Jack here some safety tips."

"Like always wash your hands before cooking!" Dad said, turning on the taps in the sink.

"Exactly!" I said, joining him.

My phone buzzed in my pocket. I glanced at the message.

WAT R U DOING? U R MAKING ME LOOK BAD.

It was from Tom. I was supposed to be gaming with him right now. I sighed and put the phone back in my pocket.

"So what are you making?" Sarah asked popping back into the room and leaning in close to me. I took a tiny step away, glancing at the ingredients. Beef mince, onions, sweetcorn…

"Er, we are making meaty-onion-corn!" I said with a grin. I heard Dad cough behind me like he had something stuck in his throat. Sarah frowned.

"Meaty," she began.

"Lasagna," Dad said. "We're making lasagna."

"Or 'Meaty-onion-corn' as my family like to call it, eh Jack?" I ruffled his hair with my hand just because I knew he hated it.

"Great!" Sarah said. "I'll leave you to it!" She winked at me and left the room. Dad sighed.

"This was a terrible idea," he said.

Tasty meaty-onion-corn

My stomach was doing flips inside me when we sat down to eat in Tom's dining room. Dad had done a great job of cooking and the steaming plates of food looked *amazing*. I was sat on one side of the table with Dad, and opposite us sat Sarah and Tom. I glanced over at Tom who looked like he was in a *bad* mood. He was staring daggers at Dad, who was too busy helping lay the table, to notice.

"Wow, this looks *amazing*, David," Sarah said.

"Thanks," Dad replied. "I worked pretty hard on it."

Sarah laughed, filling up my glass with wine. I glanced at Dad, who shook his head.

"Jack, I'm sure you made it *even better* by helping out," Sarah said. "See, Tom? If you help out more like Jack, who *knows* what you could achieve."

Tom folded his arms. "Yeah, great."

It was going terribly, so I took steps to distract everyone. I lifted up my glass of grape juice liquid. "To awesome food!" I said. "Let's eat!"

Sarah raised her glass too, tapping it on mine, as did Dad. Tom, however, just started to eat, ignoring us all. I took a sip of the wine and instantly learned that it TASTED NOTHING LIKE GRAPE JUICE.

It was *revolting*. No wonder adults were so grumpy all the time if *this* was what they had to drink. I wanted to spit it back out, but I couldn't make a scene in front of Sarah.

"Are you alright?" she asked.

I nodded, forcing the mouthful of wine down my throat. "Nice stuff," I croaked. It felt warm and strange in my stomach.

Sarah smiled again, taking a sip of her own.

As the meal went on, Sarah talked about her life and stuff and I ate the delicious lasagna. It was quite easy actually, as Sarah did most of the talking. I even drank some more wine. It didn't taste so bad the second time. Or the third time. After a while, I really began to enjoy myself. I might even say I was having a good time. I decided I would *help* Dad. After all, he wanted to date Sarah, right?

I swallowed a mouthful of lasagna and said: "You have a LOVELY smile, have I ever told you that?" I said to Sarah. It was strange. I wasn't moving, but the room seemed to be swaying from side to side.

"Oh," Sarah blushed. "Thank you."

Dad finished his meal, placing his knife and fork down. "Dad," he said quietly. "Would you like a glass. Of. Water." He said the last bit through gritted teeth.

"NO!" I said a bit louder than I had planned. "Would YOU like a gas of WATer?

Sarah laughed. "I had no idea you were such a lightweight, David."

I drank the last bit of my wine. "A white date?" I frowned. "What'sssss that?

The room spun a little. Dad started to gather up the plates. "Dad," he said, more insistently. "Why don't we go *wash up?*"

"Hmm?" I stared at the plates in his hand and back up at him and then back down at the plates. "OK then."

I waddled after Dad into the kitchen, the room spinning around me. My phone buzzed again. I looked at the screen.

`Wht is up with ur Dad???`

Another text from Tom. I giggled.

Dad shook his head. "We need to go, right now. You're making a fool of yourself!"

I folded my arms. "You're making a fool of yourself!" I said back to him in a high pitched voice. "That's how you sound, you know? Squeaky and weird."

"This is *your* voice!" Dad snapped.

"Well, you're using it wrong," I said. "And we're going when I say we're going."

I left the room before Dad could stop me going back to the dining room. If Dad wanted me to make a fool of myself, I would do *exactly* that.

Sarah was standing up now, wiping down the table with a cloth. Tom still sat in his chair, typing another text into his phone. I heard Dad following me. I walked over to Sarah and put my arms around her shoulders. She jumped slightly, before looking me in the eyes.

"Oh… hello David," she smiled. "Finished already?"

"I just wanted to say…" I hiccupped slightly. "You're really pretty and stuff. Also, your hair is really nice and I like how you speak and stuff."

Tom's eyes widened.

Dad stared at me in horror. I'd used those exact words when I asked Holly out for the first time. They *guaranteed* that the girl would want to go on another date.

"Er, thanks, David, that's really…nice," Sarah slowly stepped back from my arms and smiled. "Maybe you've drunk a bit too much, eh?"

"But," I began.

"I DON'T FEEL VERY WELL," Dad suddenly shouted. "I WOULD LIKE TO GO HOME."

I looked at him, frowning, about to tell him what a bad idea it was.

But then Sarah said, "Maybe that's for the best."

We took the bus home. I was in no state to drive, and Dad couldn't. We both sat in silence as the bus rumbled along its route.

"I don't know what to do," Dad whispered. "Everything is going wrong."

I didn't reply, but I felt exactly the same way.

No chance at the Spring Dance

This is a jk, rite?

A joke. That's what it felt like right now. I could have laughed if I wasn't feeling so down in the dumps. I forced myself out of bed, out of my room and into Dad's. I pushed open the door, fury raging in my gut.

"You asked *JASMINE* to the dance?!" I shouted.

Dad, it turned out, was also lying on his bed underneath his comforter. He groaned as I entered.

"I didn't ask her, she asked me," he said. "What was I supposed to say?"

"You say no! You say go away! You say…" I flopped onto the end of his bed. "I don't know."

We sat in silence for a moment. "She asked you? Really?"

Dad sat up. "I know, weird right?"

I shook my head. It was too late to do anything about it now. After all, it was Friday. The day of the Spring Dance. We had lied and bounced our way through the week, going from one disaster to another, trying to avoid everyone and everything. The only satisfaction we had was that tomorrow was Saturday.

"I have an idea," Dad suddenly said.

"Not another **plan**," I groaned. "They never work."

"No, an idea," Dad said, pushing back his bed covers. "This is it. We can fix a lot of the damage of the last week *tonight*." He looked at me, a grin spreading across his face. I frowned, then realized what he was suggesting.

"No." I shook my head. "No, no, no, no, no."

"Yes, yes, yes, *yes*!" Dad said, grabbing my shoulders. "This is *it,* Jack. If we go to the dance, I can make things right with Holly, and you can make things right with Sarah!"

"This is an awful idea," I said.

"We just need to apologize, say that we had an off week. They'll understand."

I didn't even reply, Dad was off in a world of his own. "If we can make things right with them, then we'll go on holiday or something. Really focus on getting this body swap thing sorted. It'll work, Jack. I know it!"

I shook my head. "You're crazy."

"Crazy AWESOME!" Dad shouted. "Come on! Let's get ready!"

When Dad came downstairs later, he was wearing the tux we had rented together for the dance. It had a cool red bowtie and when I tried it on, it made me feel like James Bond.

"How do I look?" he asked.

I looked at him sadly, remembering how excited I had been when I tried the tux on, thinking about dancing with Holly on the dance floor, imagining that it would be the night of our first kiss.

"You look great," I said quietly. I looked at what I was wearing. Dad's school clothes. Another day as the supervising teacher. "Shall we go?"

When we arrived at the school, Jasmine was waiting outside already. I'll admit, it took me a few times to realize it was her. She wore a frilly blue dress and her hair was no longer tied in braids. It flowed down in waves around her head.

I was surprised at her appearance - until she opened her mouth.

She broke into a wild grin when she saw my dad and said "Jacky!" in a high pitched squeal.

"Jacky?" I asked Dad. "Really?"

"She came up with that one," Dad frowned. "I couldn't get her to stop."

"Yeah, that's a common thing with her. Remember the idea?"

Dad nodded. "We just need to get inside fir-URST," Dad couldn't finish his sentence because Jasmine had thrown her arms around his neck and squeezed. I will admit, it was a little funny.

"Shall we go?" I grinned.

The school looked completely different to normal. The normal beige walls had been covered in large signs reading: SPRING DANCE and lots of sparkly tinsel. We could already hear the thumping music from the sports hall as we got closer.

"I'm so EXCITED!" Jasmine squealed, still clinging onto Dad's arm.

"Yeah..." Dad said, looking at me with fear in his eyes.

It was the perfect time to say, "You two have fun! I'm going in round the back!" I left Dad to fend off Jasmine in the queue of students waiting outside while I dashed around the building.

The teachers and parents who were supervising went into the sports hall through a different entrance. We didn't need tickets, after all. When I entered, the hall looked completely different to normal. It was dark, and a DJ had set up a large booth at one end. He was pumping loud music out of the speaker. Different colored lights spun around in circles, flooding the room with a cloud of color. I stood and took it all in.

"Yeah," I said to myself quietly. "This would have been awesome."

I had hoped to get to Sarah, who was also one of the parent supervisors before they let the students in, but I was too slow. Before I had even crossed the hall to the other teachers to ask where she was, students ran into the hall, screaming with excitement. I had to step around, dodging and twisting to make sure they didn't run into me.

"Woah!" I said. "Slow down! I'm- wait- careful!" Even crossing the hall was dangerous with these students running around everywhere. I stood still and tried to see what I could do. Near the entrance to the hall, I caught sight of Dad being dragged by Jasmine onto the dance floor. I shook my head. *He should be looking for Holly!* I felt frustration rising again, but I focused my search. I had to trust that Dad would do what he was supposed to.

That was when I saw the flash of Sarah, by the DJ Booth. Sarah was smiling and dancing by herself. I pushed my way through the sea of students, the music slowly getting louder and louder until I stood next to her.

"HI!" I shouted.

"I can't hear anything you're saying!" She said back.

"WHAT?" I shouted back.

"We should go over there," she pointed to the other side of the room. I nodded, pretending I understood what she meant.

We both made our way through the dancing kids, Sarah pointing at some occasionally and saying something I couldn't hear.

Finally, we reached the back.

"Hey Sarah," I said.

"David," she replied.

I took a deep breath, Dad and I had been rehearsing what we were going to say all the way here. Mine was relatively simple.

"I'm sorry," I began.

"Yes?" Sarah asked.

***

That was when Holly decided to enter the hall. She was wearing a beautiful pink dress that sparkled like a rainbow with all the lights in the hall. Her hair curled and bounced around her shoulders and I thought she looked like a princess. She was everything I had ever dreamed about and more.

She was alone. She hadn't come with anyone. She had been waiting for me to ask her.

"David? Are you OK?" Sarah asked again. I ignored her. I was looking for Dad. Where was he?

My eyes scanned the dark room. I couldn't make anything out. That was when I saw him, leaving the dance floor to walk towards her! Yes!

Followed by Jasmine! No!

He began to talk to her, but Jasmine pushed between them. She looked angry; she was shouting something at

Holly who was shouting back. My breath froze in my throat. I turned back to Sarah.

"I've got to go!" I said, pushing back into the horde of students.

"Mr. Stevenson!" Tommy Wilkins shouted, waving at me.

"Not now, Tommy!" I shouted back, continuing to push through.

Holly was trying to leave, but Jasmine grabbed her by the arm. Holly tried to shake her off and Dad stepped in between them. He waved a finger at Jasmine, trying the 'I'm very disappointed in you' face, but it failed. Holly turned and ran out of the hall.

I managed to get through just in time to see Jasmine lean in to try and kiss my dad!

Dad stepped back, horrified. "No!" he said. "That isn't what I wanted at all!"

Jasmine burst into tears. Dad looked up to see me rushing past. "Jack!" he said, but I ignored him. The idea had failed. I was on damage control now.

I burst out the front of the building and walked down the path. "Holly?" I shouted. "Holly? Where are you?" I couldn't see her anywhere. I followed the path back around the building to the yard where we had our lunch breaks. "Holly? Where…" I stopped when I saw her.

Her hair had been ruined in her attempt to escape from Jasmine. She was sitting on the bench we always sat on at breaks, staring off into the distance.

"Holly!" I said. "I found you!"

"Mr. Stevenson?" she asked, clearly confused.

I made a decision. I wanted to be *me* again. I had had enough of this.

"No," I said. "I'm not Mr. Stevenson. I'm Jack! It's me, Jack, Holly!"

Holly shifted on the bench, clearly trying to put some distance between us. "What are you saying?"

"I'm saying that…Ok, this may sound weird and crazy, and I know, because it is. Right," I took a breath. "A week ago, Dad and me, we were struck by lightning on the football field, something happened and we swapped bodies! I'm Jack! In my dad's body! You've got to believe me!"

Holly frowned. "You're…Jack?"

"Yes! Not Mr. Stevenson, not my dad, I'm me! Me!" I laughed. It felt so good to say it out loud. "I'm your boyfriend!"

"I don't understand!" Holly said, moving away even further. "You're a teacher!"

"What?" I said. "Not at all. Holly, listen."

"Jack? Where are you?" Another voice came from behind me. It was Tom! I could tell him too! He'd believe me!

"Mr. Stevenson, you're acting really creepy!" Holly stood up.

"Wait, Holly!" I tried to grab her arm, but she was too fast. She ran away.

Tom came around the corner and looked at me, confused, as Holly ran past.

"Mr. Stevenson?" he asked. "Have you seen Jack?"

I dropped to my knees, all energy leaving me. I was tired. Tired of everything.

"No," I said quietly. "No, I haven't."

In the distance, thunder rumbled quietly.

***

Find out what happens next for Jack and his dad in

Body Swap - Book 2.

Available NOW!!

If you loved Book 1 and would like to read the entire series, you can buy the full set at a discounted price.

(This is a value pack and is cheaper than buying the next 3 books individually).

Thank you so much for reading

Body Swap- Book 1

Catastrophe

If you enjoyed it, I would really appreciate a review.

Thanks so much!

Katrina

Are you ready for more laughs?

You'll love the series...

I SHRUNK MY BEST FRIEND!

Here's some more hilarious books…

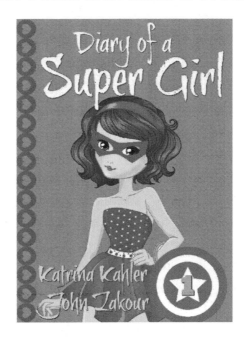

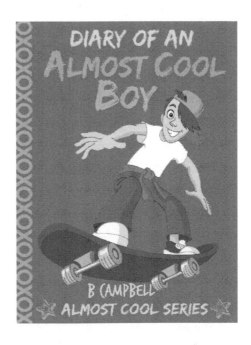

And here's some other great books that you're sure to enjoy…

Made in the USA
Middletown, DE
28 September 2018